"A BEAUTIFULLY WRITTEN NOVEL . . .
VIVID AND TOUCHING . . .
ACCOMPLISHED WITH ARTISTRY."

—*The New York Times Book Review*

"THE AGE OF WONDERS exists at the distance of
a dream, eerily couched in the language of high melo-
drama, which in Appelfeld's hands becomes the only
possible way to commemorate the stunning drama at
its core."

—*Saturday Review*

"It belongs among those rare works of fiction that
lodge in the memory more forcefully than real ex-
perience . . ."

—*The Village Voice*

"In the hands of a writer less subtle and private THE
AGE OF WONDERS could easily have become a
moral fable or a tract. Instead, the tone is plangent,
upset, vaguely bewildered; adult lunacy is accepted as
just another strange component of vanished childhood,
and that, in the end, is far more chilling."

—*The New York Review of Books*

Books by Aharon Appelfeld

The Age of Wonders
Badenheim 1939

Published by WASHINGTON SQUARE PRESS

Most Washington Square Press Books are available at special quantity discounts for bulk purchases for sales promotions, premiums or fund raising. Special books or book excerpts can also be created to fit specific needs.

For details write the office of the Vice President of Special Markets, Pocket Books, 1230 Avenue of the Americas, New York, New York 10020.

THE AGE OF WONDERS

Aharon Appelfeld

translated by Dalya Bilu

WASHINGTON SQUARE PRESS
PUBLISHED BY POCKET BOOKS NEW YORK

The author wishes to thank the Institute for the Translation of Hebrew Literature (Tel Aviv) for its generous support.

A Washington Square Press Publication of
POCKET BOOKS, a Simon & Schuster division of
GULF & WESTERN CORPORATION
1230 Avenue of the Americas, New York, N.Y. 10020

Published by arrangement with David R. Godine,
Publisher, Inc.
Library of Congress Catalog Card Number: 81-47318

ISBN: 0-671-45858-2

First Washington Square Press printing January, 1983

10 9 8 7 6 5 4 3 2 1

WASHINGTON SQUARE PRESS, WSP and colophon are
trademarks of Simon & Schuster.

Printed in the U.S.A.

BOOK ONE

1

MANY years ago Mother and I took the night train home from the quiet, little-known retreat where we had spent the summer. The coach was new, and on one of its rounded walls was a poster of a girl holding a bunch of cherries in her hand. Our places were reserved, the seats solid and comfortable with embroidered white antimacassars on their headrests. The compartment door was open and a girl, very like the one in the poster, stood there with a wooden tray in her hands. She stood in the doorway for a long time and then suddenly, as if set in motion by some external command, started walking down the aisle serving coffee and cheesecake.

The blue darkness on the windows reminded me of the quiet waters by whose banks Mother and I had spent the summer. Abandoned objects had lain scattered on the deserted banks, and the people too had seemed forsaken in the silence. There were lots of fish, small and plump, peeping up from the riverbed in mute despair. They swam slowly and bitterly, with a restlessness that infected me too.

The silence of the summer was over. Now we were on the long journey home. It too was magical, full of delicious details, such as the girl with the green silk scarf around her neck, who for some reason looked to me like a baroness. Her face against the white antimacassar was pale and transparent. Only a short while ago two servants had lifted her suitcases onto the luggage rack, and a swarthy man with a strangely elegant air had kissed her on the forehead. She had not moved a muscle since. She sat staring into space, her eyes apparently fixed on some point in the distance. Although she was partly hidden by the compartment curtain, half her face was enough for me. A stream of pleasure flowed through my limbs at the sight of her silhouette. But alas, my happiness was already flawed, created incomplete; a thin sorrow gnawed at it. The secret suspicion that this pretty face would wither before the end of the long journey shadowed my small joy. I fixed my eyes on her intently, determined not to miss the slightest movement of her face.

The white, pure, motionless face reminded me once more of the limpid days Mother and I had spent on the deserted river bank. There had been no one there but us; the people who had appeared from time to time were lost or misdirected, as I now realize—no sooner come than gone, like the breezes blowing through the bullrushes, and we had been left alone again beside the still water, shallow in the summer season. The two little fishing boats had belonged, apparently, to other days and other waters, rising in the spring. The river was meager now and its banks were dry and wrinkled. The quiet had silenced us utterly. And if in the beginning there had still been a few words trembling between us, they too had gradually died away. It was only in the water that we were together. We had come there by chance, almost caprice. Mother was sick of popular resorts and grand hotels, and Father was completely absorbed in his literary triumphs. Drunk with success, he spent his time travelling to Prague and Vienna and back again. But his successes brought us no joy. A bitter tenseness engulfed the house; it was as if we were dust to the steamroller of his success. Perhaps Father too felt no joy. Because he had gone off to Prague, Mother had decided that we would retire to some simple, desolate spot, far from everyone. And thus we had found ourselves in the rustic cabin beside the little stream that no one seemed to have taken the trouble to name. At first she had been happy, but gradually she had withdrawn further and further into herself. Her movements became fewer and a kind of stillness, as though we were under a bell jar, had enveloped us.

It was only on the last day, with all the pleasantness stripped, the two rustic beds exposed, and our suitcases ready for the journey, that Mother burst into bitter, soundless weeping. I had knelt beside her and foolishly tried to wipe her tears away. I knew that new waters had come into the river, that we had been expelled, without anyone having had to say, "Go." And all that simple splendor, consisting of no more than black bread, fresh milk, and apples in an old basket—all that simple splendor beside the nameless brook was gone forever. Mother wept and I didn't know what to say; in my embarrassment I had knelt beside her and wiped her tears away.

Now the train sailed into the darkness, gliding on its soft springs. Strange how this soft new space too seemed somehow attached to the anonymous place from whence we had just come. Every face or shadow of a face reminded me of those green waters and that rustic cabin. Perhaps even the boy who had been lifted into the front compartment in his wheelchair was already familiar to me from there. His face was very delicate, floating above the wide body that seemed to be completely paralyzed. His glance fell on me for a moment and slid off again, and I sensed that he too was full of anxiety about our silent, secret decay. Where was he going? His head floating above his broad body quietly took in every glance, every hand carefully lifting a slice of cake to every mouth. It was quite clear to me that he was thinking about us.

The feeling that we were doomed seeped through me like a thick liquid. Perhaps it was because of the appearance of the chief steward: stern and splendid in his green uniform as he passed down the aisle, asking with a cold formality if everything was all right.

"Everything's all right," said Mother. Now I understood her tears. She was afraid of this question, al-

though it had been clear from the start that it would
be asked in exactly this way. She let her hands fall onto
the armrests with an open gesture. "The steward," she
explained, "wants to know if the passengers are satis-
fied, if anyone has any special requests or unexpected
problems." She still thought there was a need for all
these explanations.

The eyes of the young baroness came alive and
darted from corner to corner. She was anxious but kept
her anxiety hidden. She smiled mysteriously. The paralyzed boy did not move. He was serene. It was as if he
had accepted his suffering and everything that would
happen to him from now on. A compassion that tran-
scended him welled up in his quiet eyes.

"Why did you leave that beautiful river bank?" He
suddenly turned his eyes in our direction.

"It wasn't our fault," I tried to drop the words silently into his questioning eyes. "New, wild waters
came down from the mountains and mixed everything
up."

"What a shame, it was a delightful place."

"There's no doubt about it, but what could we do?"

"I wouldn't have left a place like that."

And as these fantasies too gradually succumbed to
weariness, the train came to a halt. At first it seemed
like a mistake. The express didn't stop at any small
towns, much less tiny country villages. The passengers
were all so surprised that nobody moved.

But it turned out that the train had indeed stopped;
and the place wasn't even a station, but a dark old
sawmill. "We've made a wrong turn," a woman said.
"The express can make mistakes too. We're lucky not
to have been derailed." The young baroness lifted her
eyes and scanned the car with a kind of cold incompre-
hension, as if the answer to the riddle lay with us.

"Mistakes sometimes happen," said a voice from
within, very respectable.

"There've been too many mistakes lately. You can't
rely on the express any more."

The baroness was the first to rise from her place. She

pulled the window up and said to herself, "It's night. There's nothing to be seen."

"Why don't you go and inquire?" A woman turned to her husband in a nagging, provocative tone.

"What's there to inquire about? A mistake."

"You want me to do it for you?"

The man stood up and turned toward the door. He looked like a diplomat. The door opened with difficulty, creaking loudly. "For your information there's absolutely nothing to see. Just an old sawmill. Is there anything else you'd like to know?"

"Why the train stopped."

"Because the engine stopped."

"I'll never ask you for anything again," the woman spat out angrily into the air of the coach.

Other passengers lost patience and got off the train. The people looked strange next to the coaches: like little insects wrinkling the straw with their feet. Except for a woman who burst out laughing, bold laughter in a voice hoarse with cigarette smoke, the stop would have been unbearably tedious. The woman laughed and there was a kind of crazy enjoyment in her voice, as if this were what she had been waiting for all her life. The express had never been late before. This time it would be late. There was nothing more human than being late. Her husband and daughters would wait and wait. Never mind, let them wait! The thought of her husband and daughters waiting on the platform amused her and she laughed and laughed. The longer her laughter lasted the more annoying it became.

Suddenly a clear voice broke into the emptiness: express train number 422 begged the passengers' pardon for the inconvenience. Due to the special circumstances, the security forces requested all foreign passengers and all Austrian passengers who were not Christians by birth, to register at the office that had just been opened in the sawmill. Passengers were requested to bring their passports, identity cards, or any other identifying documents with them.

The coach was struck dumb, but not the laughing

woman. Her laughter grew louder, as though she had
been given too strong a drink. "That means me! A
Jewess born and bred!" The heavy, ugly laughter was
irritating in its pointlessness. Maybe it was all because
of her, maybe she had put them up to it to keep her
husband waiting. Who knew? After all, the express had
never stopped before. The commercial men, seasoned
travellers, joked among themselves.

"Why don't you shut up?" someone tried to quiet her.

"Why should I?" she retorted.

Now it was clear: her laughter was drunken. She rose
to her feet, surveyed the coach, and turned toward the
door: a fat, strong woman with a gold medallion on her
heavy bosom and mascara streaks at the corners of her
eyes. She turned her head, and for a moment it seemed
as if she were about to announce that it really was all
her doing. But to the passengers' surprise she addressed
them in a motherly tone instead, with the words:
"Come, children, let's go and register. Don't tell me
that I'm the only Jew in all this honorable company."

"Who's stopping you?" said the tall man with the
diplomatic air.

"I need company."

"Why are you talking to her?" the man's wife intervened angrily.

"Take me," the paralyzed boy suddenly said to his
companion, an elderly woman who seemed retiring and
pious.

"Where?" The old lady started up anxiously.

"To the registration office."

"What are you talking about, my boy? There's no
ramp for your chair here. You can see for yourself—
there's nothing but an open field. They only mean the
healthy ones. It's got nothing to do with you."

"I don't wish to ignore official announcements," said
the boy, giving her a piercing look.

"Of course not," said the old lady, "but you can't
deny that there are no facilities here for taking such a
heavy chair off the train. I'm only a woman after all,

and not a young one either. I can't lift a chair like that on my own."

"I'll do it," said the laughing woman. "If the boy wants to register, why deprive him of the opportunity? He's been deprived of enough in his life."

"Thank you so much for your interference," said the old lady, her voice full of suppressed anger.

"Will someone help me please?" the laughing woman appealed to the other passengers.

"I will," said the young baroness and rose to her feet.

"How funny," the laughing woman exclaimed loudly. "Who would have thought that you too belonged to our lowly race?"

The baroness did not react.

The old lady now had no alternative but to accept their help, fold the front armrest, empty the carrier, and show them how to hold the chair. She did it with ill will, mumbling and grumbling, "You'd better beware their good hearts. They'll just as soon carry you to hell."

The laughing woman took a firm grip on the chair. When she was standing outside she looked up at the coach and called maliciously, "Come out, children, come out! There's nothing to be ashamed of!"

The three women fastened themselves to the wheelchair and dragged it through the dry bushes toward the sawmill door, now illuminated by a dull electric light.

There were signs of movement in the adjacent coaches, a heavy, uneasy stir, and the sound of voices like dry laughter in the passages.

The man who looked like a diplomat lost patience, rose to his feet, and said, "I'm not hiding in here like a thief in the night. If they aren't ashamed to make such discriminatory announcements, I won't hide from them."

"Go if you want to, I'm not stopping you. But don't forget that we'll all be harmed by your actions. You're making yourself into an accomplice in this lunacy."

"What do you want me to do, ignore it?"

"That's not what I said."

"What do you want me to do, then?"

"I want you to protest. Let the people responsible know they can't do what they like. The express isn't a jungle."

"I understand. You want me to kick up a fuss."

"Do what you like. I don't feel like having an argument."

An elderly couple sitting in the corner rose from their seats. The man, who wore dark glasses, was apparently blind. The woman, small and thin, held out both hands to him with affectionate tenderness. They seemed very close. Mother immediately rose to help them, and thus we too joined the exodus.

The sawmill was in a turmoil. The instructions regarding the registration were unclear. Some practical-minded people even found advantages in the delay. One of the inspectors explained to them that nobody intended them any harm, that the registration was simply a matter of statistics. The people stood in two parallel queues. The paralyzed boy was sitting in his chair next to the counter. The laughing woman stroked his hair with maternal affection, to the annoyance of the old nurse.

Our turn came. Mother presented our papers with a very frank expression, answered for every detail, and looked at me when she gave my age, as if to stress that she had distorted nothing.

The registration came to an end. The three women dragged the wheelchair back along the length of the coaches. The boy looked pleased and helped move the stubborn wheels with his hands. The elderly couple climbed into the coach without our help. Sounds of merriment arose from the brightly lit coaches, marooned in the open field as though in the aftermath of some mischievous prank.

"Someone seems to have taken leave of his senses," said a man's voice. "I'm going to lodge a complaint."

"Yes, of course," a woman said perfunctorily, as if she hadn't actually intended to say anything.

At last the doors were locked. The passengers returned to their seats. The chief steward stood in the doorway once more, a sign that the night had returned to its former state. Only the laughing woman with the mascara streaks at the corners of her eyes kept exchanging glances with the crippled boy, who sat straight up in his chair with his hands folded in front of him.

"Anyone who didn't register can do so at the next station," the laughing woman teased the passengers. "Some of you haven't registered yet. There's nothing to be ashamed of. The Jews aren't the worst people in the world, you know. The Jews are businessmen; so what? We've got quite a few doctors too, quite a few journalists. Speaking for myself, I'm not ashamed."

"We're not here to hear your confessions," said the wife of the man who looked like a diplomat.

"I'm only trying to set the record straight," said the laughing woman, and winked at the boy.

The young baroness withdrew into her corner and stared into the distance again. The thought that she too belonged to us flooded me with a sweet sadness. The laughing woman would not let the passengers in the coach relax. She kept taking sips from a long, flat bottle and exchanging glances with the crippled boy, who sat in his chair and cut himself little squares of cake with a cold precision.

The train rushed into the night, its lamps blazing. The front coaches sounded gay and noisy, as if this were no ordinary express but one intent on merrymaking. A few couples stood in the dark doorway, immodestly embracing. The laughing woman encouraged them with all kinds of remarks and gestures. The crippled boy could not restrain his laughter.

The aggressive wife of the man who looked like a diplomat rose to her feet and said, "I can't understand what's going on here tonight. I was under the impression that this was first class, but perhaps I was mistaken."

"Don't you find our company agreeable, then?" asked the laughing woman innocently.

"No, to put it mildly."

"Sorry, but that's the way we are. What can we do about it?"

"A certain minimum of manners is required to travel first class."

"What have we done?"

"This Jewish vulgarity is intolerable."

The laughing woman jumped to her feet with a movement full of suppressed energy and said, "Look who's talking about Jewish vulgarity. I myself, for your information, am married to a gentile. I've got two daughters waiting for me now at the station, and still I haven't got the faintest wish to deny my origins—and I told my husband so, too. Not only that—I'm proud of it!"

"We haven't come here to hear your confessions. The first class isn't intended for confessions. I'm calling on the steward!"

The headwaiter appeared in the doorway and at the sight of the quarrelling women raised his right hand and said, "Ladies, come to order!"

"Call her to order!" said the laughing woman. "For your information, Mr. Headwaiter, this elegant lady is a Jewess. She took no notice of the explicit official request to register at the office. She's ashamed. What's there to be ashamed of? Aren't we human too?"

At the sound of these unambiguous words everyone fell silent.

The other woman stood up and said, "It's none of your business. I'll account for my administrative sins in full when the time comes. I'm still not in the same boat as you, thank God."

"There's nothing to hide, my lady. People are people, when all's said and done."

"I won't be lumped together with you."

"I, in any event, have nothing to hide."

"Quiet!" the headwaiter thundered. His voice was harsh and decisive, like the ring of metal on metal, and silence fell at once.

From then on not a murmur was heard. The coach

succumbed to the jolting rhythm of the train. People sat in their seats without a sound; the laughing woman let her heavy head drop to the armrest as if chastised. Smoke vapors hung listlessly in the air above the passengers' heads. Mother took my hand and said, "There's still a long way to go. Why don't you try to sleep?"

I was wide awake. The sorrow that had been dormant in me ever since leaving the river bank now broke wildly into life. In vain my mother's kind hands tried to shelter me. I knew now for sure: nothing would ever be the same again. And the place where we had spent the summer—it too was dead.

The young baroness sitting opposite us in the compartment across the aisle took off her scarf. A few tears fell from her beautiful blue-black eyes. Mother sat straight up in her seat. Her face was cold. The night breeze had frozen her expression. The headwaiter did not stir from his place in the doorway, as though he weren't a waiter at all, but a sentry posted there to keep order. The waitresses no longer served the passengers.

"What happened tonight?" I heard a woman's voice.

"Nothing. Bureaucracy gone mad."

"It frightened me very much."

"It's nothing. There's nothing to be afraid of."

The lights went out one by one. The chill of the night penetrated the coach and shrouded the people in their sleep. While the coach slept, the laughing woman rose to her feet, shook herself, took a bag of sweets from her purse, went up to the crippled boy, and said, "For you."

"Thank you," said the boy, leaning on both his hands as if he wanted to lift himself up.

"Where are you going?"

"For a reoperation."

"My poor boy, I suppose that means . . ."

"Two up to now."

"And this is the third."

"Yes."

"What courage. What heroism. How glad I am to

have met you. The people in this coach make my blood boil. I can't stand cowards. And now they're sleeping as if nothing had happened. And you, my boy, are facing your third operation. Is there any hope? What do they say?"

"They can't promise anything."

"And yet you take it so calmly, with such heroism."

"What else can I do?"

The train slowed down and the laughing woman, who for some reason now looked very fat, clutched her head in both hands and said, "What can I give this dear boy? I have nothing to give him. Here, take this medallion—it is mine." And without asking his permission she hung it around his neck. The embarrassed boy, who had been trying to support himself on his hands all this time, made a peculiar sound in his throat—a wry, twisted sound that, if it hadn't been so full of shame, might have sounded like a burst of laughter. In the end he managed to control himself and said, "I can't accept such a valuable gift. I would have to be grateful to you for the rest of my life."

"What are you saying, my boy? It's a simple gift of love. If I had more I'd give you more. You're a young hero." Without waiting for a reply she hurried back to her seat, took the narrow suitcase that seemed too small for her body, and made for the door with the words, "I get off here." The boy wanted to refuse the gift again, but he couldn't get the words out.

The train charged southward, as if it were hurtling down a hill. The boy now sat straight up in his chair with a frozen expression on his face, the gold medallion hanging on his chest. He looked as if he had been presented with a decoration he did not really want.

The nurse-companion had refrained from interfering in the conversation, but now opened her mouth and said, "You've had a windfall, my lad. It's worth thousands."

"I didn't ask for it."

"I hope you know how to appreciate such a valuable gift."

"I'm not ungrateful," said the boy angrily.

"You must admit that you didn't want to come."

"I'm not afraid. A person who's already undergone two operations has nothing left to fear."

"Nevertheless, you would have refused to come. And now see how lucky you've been!"

"What do you want of me?"

"Nothing. I'm just reminding you of the facts."

The boy hung his head and the light of the medallion flickered momentarily on his chin, a soft, boyish chin.

The noise of the engine subsided. But for the eyes of the headwaiter in the doorway it would all have seemed like an ordinary night in an ordinary summer train. The people were tired, satiated with sun and water; all they wanted was to be left to themselves and their sleep.

Suddenly, for no apparent reason, the wife of the man who looked like a diplomat turned to her husband and said, "You were wrong."

"About what?"

"You know very well."

"I don't understand you."

"You'll see."

"I haven't stolen money from the firm. I pay my taxes on time. What is my crime?"

"You're ignoring the point."

"What is the point? My dubious origins? I'm not proud of them, but I'm not ashamed either."

"No normal person would put himself into the same category as that fat cow."

"My conscience is clean."

"You can't admit your mistake, can you?"

"All right, I admit it, I admit it," he said contemptuously.

The headwaiter gave them a penetrating look and they fell silent.

The dawn broke, reminding me of all the other long summer holidays with the light of the morning sun breaking into my sleep and waking me. Something had happened this year. Perhaps because Father was not with us. And perhaps because of the strange sweetness of that deserted place, which had brought me so close to Mother, the cold realization came that nothing would last.

The morning light grew stronger and woke the passengers. They folded their blankets and exchanged glances as if waking from a nightmare that had led, in the end, to a new feeling of well-being. Mother too woke up, took the luggage down from the rack, and said absently, as if to herself, "The holiday is over."

"Will Father come to the station?" I asked.

"I doubt it," said Mother.

We managed to exchange a few more looks. The young baroness could not take her eyes off the crippled boy. A thin crease had appeared on her chin; she was still beautiful, but the softness was gone. The man who looked like a diplomat and his wife also stood looking at the boy. And for a moment there was an appealing intimacy among us, as if we had revealed ourselves to each other.

Mother took out a box of chocolates and said, "Give them to the boy."

The boy looked at me narrowly and said, "I don't need them."

"Take them!" called Mother from her place.

"I've had enough of presents."

"But the child is glad to give them to you." Mother came to my aid.

"I don't like it when people pity me."

"You're offending the child's good intentions," said Mother imploringly.

"It's not my role in life to inspire good intentions in others," said the boy.

I stood there overcome with shame.

The train slowed. We were approaching home. We stood in the doorway, and the passengers tried to soothe my small disgrace. Even the young baroness sent me a look full of sympathy. No one got off at the station but us. The kiosk was closed, with both its shutters down. The faint morning light could not hide the neglect.

"You mustn't be angry with the boy. He is very ill," said Mother. "And now he has to undergo his third operation."

We walked toward Hapsburg Avenue. We met no one on the way. The town was sunk in sleep.

"The way that woman laughed," Mother remembered.

And I felt the swaying rhythm of the train still in my feet. It would not let go of me. Nor would the people. As if we were still there, surrounded by the vapors of the night, and the eyes. But above all the steady gaze of the boy: as if it had been nailed to my forehead.

2

THAT summer with Mother has not yet left me. Sometimes it seems to me that we are still there, wrapped in the quiet waters or hurtling along the smooth tracks into the night.

As soon as we came home Mother took off her white summer dress and the secret left her face. She became very active, speaking little and moving efficiently about the house. In a few days' time we were to celebrate my birthday, and the approach of this event gave her a practical air.

Father shut himself up in his room. The summer spent between Vienna and Prague, his literary successes, made him seem tired and absent-minded.

Mother tried to distract him with all kinds of cakes and pastries, which she kept offering. And his face, always somewhat gaunt to me, grew puffy about the jaws. When Mother told him about the strange night train that had stopped to have its Jewish passengers registered, he denounced the bureaucracy at first, but immediately added that ever since the *Ostjuden* had arrived things had gone haywire. They must have brought evil spirits with them.

Day followed day. The thought that I would never return to that rustic cabin haunted me like a sad, stale smell. I was amazed at Mother, at her businesslike air: even when she came up to my room at night she never uttered an affectionate word. Her silence, which seemed to me a denial, increased my sadness.

That place was dead and everything in it, even the fishes at the bottom of the river. I felt my secret was being gradually poisoned by brilliantly colored, perfumed toxins, and at night I would wake suddenly, feeling suffocated.

In the meantime there were many feverish preparations: the house was opened up, exposed. The small domestic objects, which even then filled me with an obscure sorrow, lost their shadows and were illuminated by a harsh, probing light that had nothing to do with me. I knew that many guests, most of them unknown to me, would come and fill this void. Everyone was talking about some festivity. But I was apprehensive. Maybe because of Louise, and maybe because of the evil spirits haunting the house.

The evil spirits were many—many because intangible, appearing only in my fantasies. But sometimes they appeared in the real world too—lately in the form of the fleshly maids who had come to clean the house and assist in the preparations.

Nobody appeared to want this party, not even me for whom it was intended. It seemed to gather a momentum of its own, sweeping each of us along with its tyrannical will: Mother because she wanted to breathe a new spirit into the house, which over the past year had fallen into joyless routine; Father because his writing had reached a dead end; and me because I hoped for the unexpected. The fleshly maids had been brought in from the country, and the house was transformed into a void swept by laughter and the smells of the countryside.

They slept in the house too, and the back rooms were filled with wild laughter that invaded my sleep. A quiet, slightly suspect pleasure enveloped me, as if I were living in a transparent dream. Father stopped writing. He put on overalls and looked like a man with nothing to occupy his thoughts but odd jobs. The maids called him "master," and he stood about like an overseer dispensing favors.

By the end of the month, bright new wallpaper shone on the walls; the old sideboard had been pushed aside;

and the jarring new furniture raised the spectre of an
early orphanhood. Father paid the maids generously,
Mother added old clothes, and I was kissed with peasant lust.

And thus silence fell. Father made a list of guests.
Not all the names on the list gained Mother's approval.
The argument was bitter rather than sharp. The nights
seemed empty; only the evil spirits left behind by the
maids remained. Everything was ready for an incomprehensible freedom. An obscure terror seized my heart.

The preparations were over.

It was already afternoon and the dim light flickering
through the room made me think, for some reason, of
the fingers of a tender, transparent hand, a hand that
had invaded the room from outside, spreading its
fingers out imploringly as if to say, "Pull one vein out
of me and I'll be cured." As I stood there staring at
the flickering vision the stain appeared, a spot like a tiny
scab surrounded by an aureole of light clinging delicately to the joint of the index finger. So tangible and
transparent was the hand that I could see the flowing
movements of the molecules circling the wound. Once
more I heard, "Pull one vein out of me and I'll be
cured." Now the voice was quite clear. The hand retreated and darkness settled on the floor. In the next
room, darkened by curtains, my birthday cake stood
ready together with the violin, the music stand, and my
other anxiety. Now expectation throbbed from room to
room and stood listening outside the lavishly decorated
room of Louise, our maid.

I knew: she was standing tall and naked, making
up her eyes. In her room she was free and easy: she
had covered the walls with pictures cut out of magazines, glamour girls and famous actors. In the long
vacations when I sometimes stayed alone with her, she
would bathe me and nestle me in the big pillows of her
wooden country bed.

The violin teacher had not come yet, but I felt his
anxiety in the fingers of my left hand. My failure would
be regarded as his; but in the meantime the silence was

mine, the silence I loved to gather into myself together
with the sweet smells of the house, resurrecting as if by
magic the little pleasures of the past: the holidays, the
holidays with Louise; and the nights when I would fall
asleep with her in her bed, swooning with the odors of
powder and perfume.

The golden age was over. Now my birthday bore
the aspect of a social occasion. Louise's room was no
longer a magic shelter.

Father was in his room. In a moment he would
emerge from his retreat and fling out some threatening
word. Already the thunder of the explosion echoed in
my ears, "Where's the catalogue? Everything slips out
of my hands!" Over the past year his hair had gone
gray. He was locked in struggle with some enemy that
I, at any rate, had not met. Only with young girls was
he jocular.

"Is everything ready?" asked Mother.

"Ready," said Louise.

"Then I'll have a little rest," said Mother, and she
laid her head back on the cushion.

I went back to my room to see if the hand had come
back to claim help for its secret pain: but the shadows
had evaporated, the carpet was thick and softly padded.
I knocked on Louise's door and asked, "May I come
in?" She was standing next to the mirror, just as I had
imagined, wearing a transparent nightdress; the water
was still wet on her face. Her neck was long and arched,
like a swan rising from the water.

"Charlotte's coming tonight," she said.

"I heard."

She laughed, and her laughter betrayed everything
that lay hidden in Charlotte's name—the secret and
the suspicion.

"I don't know her," I hastened to add.

"Me neither," she whispered.

I hadn't been in her room for days. The country bed,
the pillows, the chest of drawers and the vases, everything was in its place in the feminine order I found so
attractive. A sorrow the like of which I had never felt

before suddenly closed in on me. I knew: everything here, Louise, the bed, the chest of drawers and the pillows were for some reason forbidden to me from now on.

"I haven't been in your room for ages."

"You are always a welcome guest."

But I knew, with the unerring certainty of childhood, that one of the secret cells of my being had now been violated.

"See you later," I said and shut the door.

I was tired. Playing the violin exhausted me. It was accompanied by the anxiety of my teacher, Mr. Danzig, whom Father called "a classic case of Jewish anxiety." His pedantry, which was extreme, could only be explained by the desire to punish himself—in which he undoubtedly succeeded. I liked watching his demonstrations, the way he scolded himself for his own mistakes. Even his rare smiles were only disguised grimaces of pain.

The colors of light faded and darkness flowed into the house. The armchairs were covered with a gray fuzz. I sensed that something was coming to a head in the silence. And, indeed, Mother rose and said, "It's time." Her voice sounded like a threat. She rose and, with a strange, theatrical gesture, went over to the wall and switched on the lights.

The first to arrive was Uncle Salo, with his new mistress. In an instant the silence was exploded and the salon dazzled by a harsh brilliance. He brought me an electric train, packed in two boxes, from Vienna. This mechanical marvel, which was quickly unpacked for everyone to see, raced along its narrow tracks, letting out an occasional hoot. Such were the appearances of this uncle of mine: spectacular, unrestrained, and calculated to shock the respectable. Nobody condemned his lack of decorum. On the contrary, the family would only say, "Salo doesn't live by ordinary social conventions." Of course, he didn't always get away with it. There were various scandals. But his wife was not thought very bright and perhaps that was the reason they forgave him his escapades.

We drank tea. Perfumed smells drifted in from Louise's room—a sign that her toilette was nearing completion. The door opened. Louise appeared in a pleated flowered dress, her face all rouged and shining. And Uncle Salo, who admired women in general, rose from his place and announced, "See what's been hiding here." His new mistress was embarrassed, an expression of strained liveliness about her mouth. The family jargon was strange to her. Of course, everyone talked about Charlotte, her attractions and successes, and the hard times upon which she had fallen of late. Whispered remarks were exchanged that I failed to understand. One thing I knew: there was something dark at the heart of this affair.

At the appointed time my Uncle Karl appeared with his wife. Immediately everyone seemed to freeze. He was a lawyer, correct in his behavior and sensitive to the quirks our family displayed in abundance. Not so his wife, who was younger than he and who allowed herself a certain freedom in her manners. Their marriage wasn't all smooth sailing either, but it was a struggle that had been going on for years without, for some reason, ever exploding. His relations with his high-spirited brother too alternated between anger and conciliation; but because the ties between the brothers were very strong, their quarrels were acrimonious. This time, however, he ignored Salo and sat down in a corner.

The gaiety was not affected. More guests mustered at the door, and Father put on the expression of affable host.

How wretched my teacher Danzig looked among the guests! Even when he sipped his coffee and nibbled a piece of cake the trembling of his shoulder did not leave him. Nobody asked him how he was, and the way he sat there on the edge of his chair filled me with desolation.

My turn came and I affected a self-confident expression. Danzig, standing by my side, seemed to shrink. "Wide bow, wide . . ." he whispered distractedly.

The first part went successfully. In the second part my fingers betrayed me horribly. Danzig's face changed color; in the end he covered his face. No one blamed me. My weakness, exposed to all eyes, gave rise to an indulgent sympathy; but this was not the case with my teacher Danzig, who saw every flaw in my playing as his own. The merriment was at its height, and no one took any notice of his disappearance. I was the talk of the party. My talents were attributed partly to my father. Of the grave defects in my playing I was as well aware as my teacher, but I pretended there was nothing wrong. Uncle Salo's new mistress clutched my hand. Her understanding of music was not great, but she had evidently been charmed by my posture.

Everybody was waiting for Charlotte. They said, "She's probably not coming." Mother cut the strawberry cake with her own hands. Louise served it as if she were floating. It was already nine o'clock and Uncle Salo started demonstrating his freedom by drinking excessively. The band, which was late due to the pouring rain, stationed itself on the platform. Uncle Salo held his mistress as lightly as a boy. Uncle Karl surveyed the room sternly, took his wife by the hand, and said, "Come on, let's go." She gave us the despairing look of a person suddenly dragged from her pleasures into the cold black night. But there was no help for it.

The band gave rise to a different intoxication. How strange Father looked sitting in his chair, chatting to the lawyer Landmann about some family property leased to strangers in his hometown. The look in his eyes was serious and contemplative, as if they were discussing not some obscure legacy but his secret inner life. The lawyer took the opportunity to feed him with facts and figures.

Suddenly everyone seemed struck dumb. Uncle Salo's gesticulating hand froze in midair. His mistress too lost her silly look. Her eyes were grieving and astonished. Father asked loudly, "What will become of the land?"

as if he understood that there was no real hope. The lawyer did not reply.

"Is there anything wrong with the cakes?" asked Mother in despair.

The band played sentimental songs. Father, who couldn't stand this sweetness, said nothing. Perhaps it was Mother's desperation that silenced him, her stricken attempts to gather a few crumbs of attention. What's happened? her face asked again. Nothing, it seemed. Only a fleeting, impalpable stillness as the people stopped talking and sank into the flowing vacuity of the music. Louise came in with a tray of fresh coffee, her ruddy face full of life.

Uncle Salo reached for the cognac bottle with his pale hand and poured himself another glass. Doctor Herz Brauer sat in a broad armchair, the upper half of his body immobile. From the day of his wife's death, a pillar of clouds had divided him from his fellows, and when he sank into a chair the clouds grew denser and covered his whole face. And when he stood up, the clouds stood with him. He liked saying, "There's more to it than meets the eye"—a phrase that had remained with him from the golden age of his flourishing private practice. Mother offered him his favorite cheesecake. But Dr. Brauer did not stir. "Won't you taste a little, Dr. Brauer?" Mother's voice was imploring. Doctor Brauer stirred and said, "Right away," and stuck his fork into the cake.

"Charlotte won't come now," they said. "She never goes out so late." Uncle Salo filled more glasses, and his mood grew jovial. He scurried between the salon and the dining room, helping Louise carry the trays. His new mistress was not pleased with his behavior and said, "You've had too much to drink. Why don't you sit down?" But helping Louise to serve entertained him too much for him to stop.

His joviality did nothing to lift the gloom. Father rose from his chair and stood next to the lawyer Landmann, lecturing him about the leased land, a legacy from his parents, with a pathos unfamiliar to me. No one listened to him. And to me it seemed that he was talking angrily about himself. Uncle Salo was far gone. He was completely drunk, holding forth about the greatness of our family. One by one he counted the musicians, painters, and writers, the converts and the international speculators. The incessant flow of words and names tickled the roots of the sadness a little, but did not bring relief.

Someone said that anti-Semitism was raising its head again, but Uncle Salo embraced Louise and said, "Tell us, don't you love the Jews? Is there anyone better in the world? Aren't they the greatest lovers? Tell us, Louise, tell us!"

"They are, they are," said Louise, and blushed to the roots of her hair.

"There you are!" said Uncle Salo.

"Yes, but what about Charlotte? Haven't you heard that they've fired Charlotte from the National Theatre? Hasn't that rumor reached your ears yet?" cried one of the industrialists.

"Why? Why?"

"Because she's Jewish, that's why."

"I can't understand it. I can't understand it," said Uncle Salo, and held on to the tray.

And while everyone stood spellbound the door opened and the great Charlotte, the illustrious Charlotte came into the room. So unexpected was her arrival at this point that everyone, including the band, fell silent in their places. Only Uncle Salo called out, "Charlotte!"

Now I saw: her face glowed with a strange light. She dominated people easily. I did not know then how intimately involved she was with our little family, and how entangled her life was with ours.

Charlotte pulled the party out of its well of apathy. Coffee was forgotten. The guests drank brandy. Words I had never heard in our house before flew through the air. It was already late, but no one said, "It's time to go." And Louise too, I noticed, had a smile budding on her closed lips.

"And what has Charlotte got to say for herself?" said Salo, perhaps for no better reason than to hear the sound of his own voice. Charlotte, already drunk when she arrived, said with a charming arrogance, "I'm celebrating my new freedom. Pull up your chairs and drink a toast to Charlotte's new freedom!" I sensed: my own little life, held to its narrow compounds, had escaped from its constraints and approached the threshold of a darkness I did not understand. Charlotte cursed in a manner I had never heard in our house before. To my astonishment, nobody blushed. The sparks in her eyes no longer hid their rage. Everybody went on drinking. Uncle Salo's new mistress overcame her embarrassment and laughed wildly. Charlotte cursed the barons and directors and actresses shamelessly. Advocate Landmann suddenly stood up and said in a quiet voice, "This is incomprehensible."

"Doesn't Advocate Landmann regard himself as an equal member of the honorable Jewish order then?" hissed Charlotte.

"No."

"In that case, what is the honorable advocate doing at our central committee meeting? Wasn't he elected of his own free will?"

"No."

"If so,"—she turned to Salo—"Advocate Landmann questions the legality of his election. What says the charter?"

"Madame Secretary, hand over the charter," said Salo to his new mistress.

"There's no need for that," said Landmann angrily. "This madness has nothing to do with me."

"You're a Jew. You can't get out of it. Your parents had you circumcised, didn't they? They stamped you with the noble seal. You're not trying to deny that glorious birthmark, are you?"

"What vulgarity."

"Why vulgarity? A simple, modest fact of life."

"I don't want to talk about it."

"What's the matter?"

"I'm a human being."

"Of course. But one who carries a certain distinguishing mark on his flesh, you must admit."

"Vulgarity."

"Salo, cross him off the register! The order declares him lost, irretrievably lost!"

The merchant Brown took advantage of the uproar to drag Louise off to her bedroom. This did not, apparently, go unnoticed by the others, but no one seemed prepared to make a fuss over a bit of adultery at this point. Especially since it was a well-known fact that the merchant was not one to miss any opportunity that came his way.

The commotion reached a climax. Landmann turned to the door and thundered, "I will not be a party to this madness!"

"Cross him off the register, Salo!" shouted Charlotte.

"The charter calls for a vote."

"No need, this is a clear case of contempt." Charlotte's face was red. She said anything that came into her head. My little pain tightened inside me, and the more her voice swelled the more it seemed to me that it was my own. Words I did not understand flew through the air like flaming torches. And while I was trying to gather up the courage to break into Louise's room, Charlotte threw a bottle at the front door. In the end, they separated the combatants. They took Landmann into the passage and led Charlotte into the library. Brown slipped away by the back door.

About an hour later Louise came out of her room to remove the dirty dishes from the tables, her face flushed and an excited smile on her lips.

Charlotte refused to spend the night at our house and Father led her swaying to the taxi. "Darling." She turned to me, as if I were another object amid her wild thoughts. It was raining and cars buzzed like hornets down the wet road. Inside, silence seeped through the rooms like a liquid about to jell. Suddenly I sensed Charlotte's drunk little face and her lost look directed, trembling, at my forehead, and my father's hand, as if it were touching me, not her. Uncle Salo dragged his new mistress down the stairs. She was neighing like a horse. Uncle Salo said, "Give me a hand or a leg." His mistress was convulsed with laughter.

The scenes of the night came pouring out of me as if they were about to plunge over a precipice. A few shallow words still hung in the air together with the last notes of the band. I knew: dark seeds, seeds that already had pinkish roots, had been planted in me that night.

The rooms were messy, rumpled. Mother sat in an armchair, her eyes closed.

A bright, harsh light poured from the chandeliers and penetrated shamelessly into all the corners.

The next day the rooms were cleaned, but the evil spirits lingered on. Although no one spoke, it seemed to me that everything we did was governed by the jangling rhythm of Charlotte's words. Louise wore a knitted blouse and her two big breasts exuded an air of importance.

3

THE end of summer we spent together in a country cottage near Baden. It was an ancient village with many water wells, lawns, and a church with a small hall. The light lingered until late at night in a thin and drenching pattern. And the evenings were green and dense with moist country smells. Nobody ever said, "It's getting late"; night fell as slowly as at the seashore and the days died only when I shut my eyes in sleep.

For the first time I saw the youngest of my aunts, Theresa. She was seventeen, tall and very like Mother. Even then there was a pure kind of light hovering about her forehead. She was preparing for her matriculation examinations, and these examinations seemed to me, for some reason, a late childhood disease that attacked people when they were seventeen years old. At dusk she would emerge from her room and put on her jacket, like a prisoner whose hours are measured out for him. And when she came back she would sit with Mother and Father in the rustic parlor; but these hours no longer belonged to me, they belonged to my sleep. Dimly the outline of her face would reveal itself to me, and immediately dissolve, seeping into me like a sweet, soft touch.

There were some frightening shadows too, like Dr. Mirzel who appeared with the evening and pinched my cheek and said, "Here's a little Jew for you."

"Why Jew?" Mother would protest.

"Because of the child's pale looks. Boys should be toughened up when they're young."

Father would emerge from the inner room and call out, "Doctor Mirzel, where are you?"

"Wherever I go I'm surrounded by Jews, there's no escaping them!" Dr. Mirzel would joke.

I knew this was nothing but jocular evening mood. But still, it left a disagreeable feeling that crept into my sleep at night. The bright morning would come and wipe it all away, especially when it began with a walk along the river bank and ended at the flour mill where colored bottles of cider were sold in the cellar.

But the one who really cast a spell on that summer's end was Father's stepmother. She was already ninety-three years old, blind, and had been forgotten in a sanatorium for the last thirty years. None of us ever mentioned her name. I don't think we really wanted to see her again. But it happened without our consent. A letter arrived from the sanatorium in the nurse's handwriting sending greetings to us all and couched in terms to which we were not accustomed: "I think of you often and I often see you in my dreams." Father hurried to show the letter to Mother. They looked at each other, and Father said, "Strange, isn't it?" And on the spot he decided to take the old lady with us to Baden.

From then on there was a certain routine to events. Father sat out together with Uncle Salo, and we stood at the window waving gaily. But an obscure uneasiness stole into my heart.

The arrangements, as usual, were muddled, and Mother and I set out late. In the end we arrived at the station on time. I was sorry that Louise wasn't coming with us. Louise, at this time, held a sweet, secret fascination for me, and my sorrow at her absence clouded my small happiness.

When we arrived at Baden it was night. The platform was overflowing with lights. Next to the kiosk men and women crowded together, clutching each others' hands. The warehouses were already closed, and next to them stood horses with shackled legs.

At the exit Father and Uncle Salo were waiting for us with the invalid bed between them. On the bed lay Father's stepmother, Amalia. We spoke to her. "She's very quiet," said Uncle Salo, as if he were talking not about a human being but about some rebellious creature now subdued. We had to take a double carriage, harnessed to four horses. At first she didn't recognize our voices, and refused to go with us. But we coaxed her and promised her pleasant company. Father's face was very strange. It was as if he were not party to this adventure, and everything was happening because of some hidden command. He took on a kind of helplessness, and a sheepish, baffled look I had never seen in him before.

Grandmother Amalia had daughters from a previous marriage, and they had taken care of her needs at the beginning. But in the course of time they had married gentiles and lost touch with her. In recent years no one had come to visit her. All this Father and Uncle Salo had heard from the nurse, a nun who had become very attached to the old lady.

The first days of the holiday were pleasant, as usual. Louise was summoned from the house and entrusted with the care of Amalia. Between one walk and the next we would peep in to see that everything was all right. A doctor came from Baden and pronounced, "An admirable old lady." And thus the long days overflowing with light came back to us. Once a day Father and Uncle Salo took her cot out onto the lawn. Then I saw it close up: an upraised stretcher standing on four clawed feet, unnecessarily ornate and reminiscent of some ancient ritual object. Actually, it was nothing but an old-fashioned chest with four carved table legs stuck to its corners, and the work was so slipshod you could see the joints at a glance.

For a few days she lay curled in her bed without uttering a sound. Her blind face expressed no desire or pain. Uncle Salo said proudly, "An admirable old lady," and the next day he went off to Vienna. Father returned to his proofs.

Even then a few ominous signs filtered in, but they were too faint to disturb the predetermined order of our lives. Aunt Theresa studied diligently. To me, for some reason, it appeared a bitter asceticism. Once a week she would go off to take an exam and when she returned her brow was clouded, the hollows of her eyes dark, and her hair dry and tangled. She would immediately shut herself up in her room again. Mother said that in her time they were even stricter. Still, nothing was spoiled: the walks, the sailing on the river, the light meals at inns, and in the evening, dinner at home. The National Theatre was dramatizing one of Father's stories, and the project brought us new friends. But the gay evenings did not always end on a happy note. Father was a sworn devotee of Franz Kafka. Kafka's few published works had converted him completely. He knew them all by heart. The arguments about Kafka would sometimes go on until late at night. It was then that a word struck my ears for the first time: decadence. But these arguments, to tell the truth, belonged to my sleeping rather than my waking hours.

"Where are we?" Amalia woke from her blindness.

"Not far from Baden, in an ancient village. Fresh air and lots of wells."

"And Jews?"

"Apart from us, I think not."

"Strange," said Amalia, "I thought there were Jews here."

"You've forgotten Dr. Mirzel," said Mother.

"Yes, Dr. Mirzel is a Jew born and bred."

Ever since she had lost her sight Amalia had stopped eating cooked food and she subsisted on salads. Her daughters had tried to talk her out of it at first but nothing helped. She was suspicious of cooked food. She took leave of all her old habits and entered her blindness with new ones. During the period of her blindness, and it was a long one, there was never any demand for special food—she kept to salads.

The quiet of the village immersed us in its summer softness. Once a week we would go into Baden, where

the tourists swarmed around all the pavement booths.
Father couldn't bear the place and called it a hornet's
nest of petit-bourgeois Jews. They weren't really Jews
any more; all that was left of their Judaism was the
desire to go on eating and making a noise together.

When we came back from Baden Father would barri-
cade himself in his room with his proofs. His books
were coming out one after the other. He had some
enemies, of course, who never missed an opportunity to
get at him, but they were minor. The critics praised
his books. At this time Father became very close to
Stefan Zweig. Sometimes they spent whole days together in Vienna.

"And how is our Amalia today?" Uncle Salo would
inquire lightheartedly.

"Everything's all right," Louise would reply.

One day Amalia asked to be propped up into a
sitting position. Her box-bed was fitted with a kind of
lever for raising its upper part. We all labored to turn
the handle, which had rusted from disuse, and in the
end we succeeded. Amalia rose from her box and sat
up.

For the first time we saw her blind face. It was a
small face, shrunken into concentration by the years.

She asked everyone's name.

Father introduced us briefly without going into detail.

"And don't people pray here?" she asked.

"No," said Father, surprised.

"I heard the sound of praying."

"This is a little village, not far from Baden."

"My ears are deceiving me again," she said, angry
with herself, and fell silent.

Mother went to prepare supper, Louise let the bed
down, and Amalia sank into the box without a word.

We had guests for dinner: Dr. Mirzel, two actors,
and a lady writer with a gay manner. After about an
hour I fell asleep on the bench in the hall. My sleep
that night was strange: I had lost everyone and retreated into myself as into the silence of high-growing
reeds.

The next day it rained and we were outside in the fields in light summer clothes. Father opened his arms as if calling upon the rain to wash him. Mother smoothed her wet hair and her face became young again. Because the rain was coming down harder we ran toward the nearby farm. Father shouted, "It's a flood!" It was a mushroom farm, mushrooms for export. The farmer greeted us coldly and said, "Unseasonable rain this year." We went home wet.

For two days Theresa did not show her face. She was afraid of the Latin exam. Mother sat with her and helped her learn passages by heart. Louise came into the parlor and announced, "Amalia enjoyed her supper tonight. She prayed and fell asleep." Louise had a strange, pious expression on her face: as if she was looking after a living statue rather than a human being.

And while we fortified ourselves with our daily routines, the lawn was cut, the late cherries appeared, and Theresa passed her exams with flying colors. While we all sheltered in the tranquil shade, Amalia started muttering silently to herself. At first Louise thought that she didn't like the food, but the trouble wasn't the food—it was the noise. She said that the birds made a noise in her head at night. Father stood by her bed and explained: they were ordinary birds, quiet country birds, birds without any evil intentions, who were apparently migrating to places with more water at this time of year. Amalia did not agree. They were not local birds. The noise they made was not in the least like the noise of country birds. She spoke confidently, as if she had firsthand knowledge, but to us it seemed like the hallucinations of blindness. How surprised we were when the next day a large flock of birds appeared in the sky and none of us was able to identify them. Even the landlady, a native of the village, did not know them: and when Father told Amalia, the two slits of her eyes opened momentarily, as if smiling, and closed again.

From then on she never stopped complaining. She grumbled about the noise, about the salad greens that weren't proper salad greens, but above all about her two daughters who had married gentiles and converted. God would not forgive them. How could he possibly forgive them? And now she could not die because of them.

"It's not your fault. . . ." Father tried to say something soothing.

"Of course it's not my fault."

"Why are you torturing yourself?"

"Because I can't die. How can I depart this world when my daughters have apostasized?"

There was power in her voice: next to her we felt small. Her mouth was a dark crater erupting words whose certainty was forged of steel.

"What would you like us to do?"

"What can you do?"

Because it was raining and impossible to return her to the sanatorium, we were forced to spend a whole week listening to her complaints and heartfelt bitterness. From day to day her voice grew louder, her memory came back to life. But strongest of all were her beliefs: these were harsh and vengeful. God would have no mercy on apostates. They would never be at peace. Not here and not in the worlds to come. All of her and our apostates stood lined up in a row in her head, and she never tired of repeating their names.

And because words were of no avail and her complaints grew louder, Father decided there was nothing to do but send her back to the sanatorium. The next day her bed stood outside the door. The carriage arrived on time and without consulting her, we set out.

All the way to the sanatorium she spoke to herself. Now it was clear that she was no longer sorry for herself, but for her daughters, for the harsh judgement awaiting them in the world to come. We sat in the train and Father tried to cover up our disgrace.

At the sanatorium the procedure was brief. The nun who looked after Amalia was glad to see her, and we said good-bye and left. We were embarrassed and confused, as if we were running away from something shameful.

The rest of the holiday we spent indoors. Theresa studied all the time and Mother helped her. After every exam a pink line was etched on her lips, but she sat for them all at the appointed times and passed them all. The glory of the summer's end was complete, the sky flawless. But for the echo of Amalia's voice, which would not go away, the vacation would have come quietly to its end.

Louise kept on repeating, "I don't know what Amalia did to me. She changed me—or something; I don't understand."

"It's nothing," Mother comforted her.

"I can't sleep," complained Louise.

Doctor Mirzel went back to his mother and we threw a little party for him. Again he called me a little Jew who needed to be toughened up on the sports field. Theresa did not attend the party.

Louise found herself a boy friend and went out with him. Since Amalia's departure she could find no peace in the house. Late at night she would come back flushed and dishevelled and immediately burrow into her blankets. One night she broke into bitter weeping. "Ever since Amalia left us I've been sinking into the gutter. The men are eating me up. What will become of me?"

Mother comforted her. "Soon we will be going home and you will forget everything." But she would not be comforted. She was tortured by a blind, obscure sorrow and could not stop talking about Amalia. As if she had lost not only her youth, but also her household gods. That same autumn she left us.

4

IN the autumn Father set out for the provincial capital to take part in a court case concerning the forgotten inheritance, an old, ugly affair that gave him no rest and that he had decided to settle once and for all in the law courts. But this move apparently only complicated matters.

His literary successes had begun to sour. One of his publishers had demanded cuts and complained that the manuscript was wearisome and too long. Father, I remember, was very upset; but in the end, as usual, he found that the man was right. There was a flaw in the structure—to be precise, many flaws. The style too was far from perfect. For weeks he had worked on corrections. In the end, he was still dissatisfied. He wrote a long, apologetic letter and asked for the manuscript back.

Just about that time, the ugly old business of the inheritance came up again, and he decided to go to the provincial capital and get that affair, at least, out of the way. Perhaps a successful campaign in the courts would make his humiliation at the hands of his publishers easier to bear.

But the way things turned out, there were many claimants to the small inheritance, aggressive claimants with sharp lawyers. For a week we heard nothing from him, and at the end of the week Mother set out after him in a panic and I was left alone with the new maid, a tall woman with pale, northern eyes, pedantic and humorless.

All of a sudden my days became cold and orderly. At night the cold light rested mercilessly on my bed. The new maid had apparently been previously employed in tall, isolated houses, and she had brought their chill with her.

One evening my violin teacher Danzig appeared at our door. He had grown taller, thinner, and his striped suit, once so well pressed, hung flapping and crumpled on his back. The new maid was about to send him away like a beggar, but I insisted he be shown in and given a cup of coffee. At first she refused, but when she saw my determination she agreed. And then I saw how he had changed. His face was lost, and the slight trembling of his left shoulder had spread to his hand, so that the long fingers, which had once conveyed delicacy and restraint, now twitched in time with his shoulder.

He was about to sail for Australia, but before leaving Europe he wanted to come and apologize to us. It was all his fault. Some hidden flaw, some defect he was incapable of locating, was ruining his playing. We sat in the salon and he told me about his parents, middle-class textile merchants who had worked for him all their lives and sent him from one academy to another and from one maestro to another in order to correct the faults that had crept into his playing. At first it seemed he would be able to root them out and perhaps even derive some new power from them. But it was an illusion. Something in his fingers, perhaps something in himself, prevented him from attaining perfection. And so he decided, on the advice of his late mother, to become a violin teacher for the children of the rich, but one day he suddenly realized that he was transferring his own faults to his young pupils.

"And do you still play yourself?" I asked.

"No."

I wanted to make him happy and I didn't know how. I showed him my report card and Father's latest book, which had been highly praised. The new maid sat in

the kitchen and listened. I saw she was annoyed by the
presence of the poor man in the salon. But I was happy.
As if a clearly written page of life had suddenly been
revealed to me, I talked a lot and told him about
Theresa who was now doing well at the Academy of
Art in Vienna. His still, dark face seemed to come
alive for a moment and look at me with compassion.
Now I knew: the little flaws, which could not be
rooted out, had turned into open wounds, and now he
was taking them with him far away to Australia.

I told him about Louise. At one time Danzig had
also accompanied us on our long vacations, bringing
his violin and playing for us. And although he had
been something of a shy bachelor even then, we had
occasionally seen him in the company of a young village
girl. He would often complain about the defects in his
playing and Father would advise him jokingly, "Marry
a country girl, my friend, or convert, and your defects
will vanish in the twinkling of an eye. Jewish sentimentality is no good for art."

The maid brought him a cup of coffee and a slice of
stale cake and Danzig buried his face in the cup. My
words were cut off inside me and I didn't know what to
say or how to make him happy. His face buried in the
cup rendered me speechless.

"Why don't you stay with us? My parents would be
very glad to have you."

"There's no going back. I have to be in Vienna tomorrow."

I knew that I was powerless to help him, but nevertheless I went on imploring him to stay. There was
nothing else I could do. Danzig stood up and said, "I
have to go." The evening light was fading and I stood
at the door, bereft even of my sorrow.

The next day my parents returned from the provincial capital bringing with them a breath of alien
tumult, words and phrases they had picked up in the
law courts. I understood nothing, but this I knew: they
were still there. Father took off his winter shoes and

scattered his clothes all over the salon, everything about him expressing the distraction of a tired businessman. Mother kept defending the chief witness who had appeared in the case. And when I told them that Danzig had come the night before and that he was on his way to Australia, Father said, "Who?" Neither did Mother ask for any details; they were both so absorbed in the court case that it was impossible to draw them into anything else. Father cursed the little Jews who could think of nothing but money and who stirred up strife wherever they went. Their dark avarice drove them crazy.

That night I felt my own little loneliness deep inside me. Now I knew: the quiet, still days that had filled the rooms of the house with the serenity of small activities, those days were over.

For days on end the house was preoccupied with the court case. Father never stopped talking about the hostile witnesses and unfair judges. Although they never mentioned Amalia's name, it seemed that her imprisoned voice was beating between the double windows and that the reflection of her face would not disappear even in winter.

Theresa was already deep in her academic studies and her beautiful letters filled us with emotion. She was doing very well, but she did not seem overjoyed by her success. Her letters contained an abundance of detail that showed great perceptiveness. Father would exclaim admiringly over her precise descriptions, which were not lacking in a sly sense of humor. She herself seemed outside the teeming academic world. To our surprise we learned that even during the difficult summer months she had not missed a single detail of the events unfolding around her—the arrival and departure of Amalia, for example, or Uncle Salo's eccentricities, or Louise's sexual agonies. And thus from a distance she became very close to us. Who could have guessed that within that clear soul the dark jungle drums were already beating?

5

I REMEMBER the night train home from Baden
clearly. In every year of my childhood we took the
same train home, and every year I heard the night,
murmurous with pleasure and fear, whispering in my
ears. But above all I remember this journey, our mad
flight through the night with Mother's younger sister,
Theresa, whose face, in the middle of our holiday, had
suddenly been overshadowed by a secret passion, pale
and consuming, that gradually had spread until it
covered her neck. For several days she had said nothing, as if fallen into a waking sleep. And when she
came to, sharp wrinkles had appeared in her cheeks.
Her pursed mouth had muttered words I did not understand. But one thing I knew: this was no longer the
place for her. A pure, frightening beauty had shone
from her smooth forehead. Mother hurried to pack the
two colored suitcases. The green, radiant, summer light
was transformed into an ugly autumn cloud.

The sun shone and we stood waiting in the dark back
entrance of the pension. Father took the headwaiter
aside and whispered confidentially to him. Even the
carriage that came to take us to the station was far
from grand. It was a plain coach harnessed to two
skinny horses, as though we had suddenly lost all our
money. Father strode ahead of us with his coat open
for some reason, as if he were trying to dismiss our
disgrace from the world.

"Go!" said Father, using the country dialect.

46

The coach turned onto an unpaved road leading into the industrial district, where we had never set foot before. And if there was still any doubt in my heart, here were the wretched, gloomy houses next to the sugar factory to prove that the holiday had not ended naturally, with the elegant, expansive ease I was accustomed to in previous years.

In the winter months, prior to our harrowing journey from Baden, Aunt Theresa had been hospitalized in a well-known sanatorium, St. Peter's, due to her recurrent depressions. In the house her name was whispered with a kind of hidden awe. Every week Mother would travel to the sanatorium. She had a special coat and special hats for this trip, and when she came back a strong light shone from her forehead. I never asked what it was like there or anything of that kind. It was agreed between us that I asked no questions. And lo and behold, in the springtime Theresa suddenly appeared amongst us—tall and young and sometimes very like Mother, even in the way she sat in the armchair. You couldn't see any special signs on her face. Her long dresses suited her figure. A fine, mild spring flowed in the streets, and in our house, too, happiness reigned. Father's fourth book had come out, and it was a success. Two journals praised his style and said that he had brought to Austrian literature a beauty that was sickly, but nevertheless new. Stefan Zweig sent a letter of congratulation, and Father's success smiled on us too. Judges, lawyers, and doctors, looking for a little intellectual stimulation in the calm provincial backwaters, made frequent visits to the house.

But the spring belonged to Theresa. Her face in the evening, when she sat by the stove in her long dress, was the embodiment of religious spirit in a woman's form. Mother never left her side for a moment. She said not a word about her life in the sanatorium, but all her movements, long and graceful, spoke of evening breezes, tall trees, and a life aspiring to inwardness. And we too were captured by this quiet splendor. The spacious rooms drank the light in thirstily. Two flowered umbrellas were taken out to the verandah, and although we had no maid at the time our evening meals were always fresh and decked with greenery.

The nights too seemed purged of little aggravations. Father's voice washed my ears with clear words very easy to understand, such as, "Let's pick the corner table up together and take it out on to the verandah. The spring sky won't disappoint us." Or Mother, always unsure of herself, as if she could never do anything right, would venture, "Perhaps the wicker chairs?" And the little domestic arrangements seemed to bring me momentarily closer to the odors of an ancient ritual, one we had long forgotten but were now reviving on a small scale.

The summer came and Theresa's face showed no signs of anything wrong. In her tight summer jacket she looked like a student again, one whose studies had left a certain appealing weariness in her gestures. As for me—school was over. The time was ripe to set out. The gentle transition, accompanied by all its preparations, had a special festivity this time. Theresa blossomed inwardly, giving rise to thoughts of very quiet places where she had dwelt. The tranquility she had absorbed there never left her face, even when she laughed. And suddenly—while we were immersed in the scenery and the intoxication of the light floating down the river, all open to the sun—the pale, consuming, secret passion appeared on Theresa's face and spread to her neck and slender fingers, and she fell into a state of waking sleep.

Stunned, we stood and watched her as if we were looking at the face of fear itself. Mother sank to her knees, clung to Theresa's hands, imploring her, "What is it? What is it?" And when words failed to help, Father paid the bill and spoke in whispers to the headwaiter with a panic-stricken expression on his face. And then we went out of the dark back entrance into the sinking day.

We reached the station at dusk. The timetable had been changed and we had missed the express. There was nothing for us to do but wait in the narrow tunnel of light and steam for the next train. Now I saw: grimy tanks hung on pipes underneath the riddled roof, making an ugly humming noise.

Father smoked one cigarette after the other and his eyes darted about, as if he wanted to hide us on the ugly bench standing by itself on the first-class platform. Mother, for some reason, was wearing her winter raincoat. Not far off, in a warehouse, joined to the train coaches by a ramp made of planks, shackled horses were being led out in pairs, blindfolded by sacks. The horses groped their way forward on the sagging planks, stumbling and rearing as they shied away from the whip of the groom roaring from the warehouse door. As soon as they had crossed the bridge, the second groom, standing next to the coaches, cracked his whip down on their flanks; the horses reared up on their shackled legs and collapsed into the boxlike coach. For a moment the bridge was empty, the grooms exchanged glances, and the next pair of horses, shackled and blinded, came out of the warehouse door.

A different darkness fell from the roof and the horses vanished from my sight. Father asked if anyone wanted lemonade.

And in the meantime people collected on the rear platform. The caged lightbulbs illuminated the wet floor. For some reason it seemed to me that in a moment or two the blindfolded horses would break out of the box and trample the people on the platform. Not far off, next to the kiosk, a different group gathered, dressed in strange black and striped garments. They devoured sandwiches greedily.

"Who are those people?" asked Theresa.

Her question, apparently, was not heard.

"Who are those people?" she asked again.

Mother bent down and whispered, "Jews," as if she were explaining an incomprehensible word picked up on the streets.

"Lately they've been appearing in droves," said

Father, rather overloud. Then he immediately added to himself, "We'll get something to drink on the train."

Theresa's looks now brightened, and she concentrated on the Jews as if she wanted to catch them in the beam of light coming out of her eyes. Suddenly she giggled and said, "They're eating sandwiches."

The lovely holiday, all woven of trees and water, suddenly shrank here in the cold darkness, leaving only this narrow strip of floor slotted by weak rays of the caged bulbs. Porters were sitting next to the counter smoking. Their grimy faces bespoke dull futility.

"Who are those people?" asked Theresa again.

"Jews," said Mother.

"Where are they going?"

"I don't know."

They were always talking about Jews at home, but always in a lowered voice and with a kind of grimace. And sometimes in an outburst, "You can't deny it, we too are Jews." Ever since Father had discovered Martin Buber, this little disgrace had found a certain if incomplete remedy. A few years before Father had gone off to Frankfurt to meet Buber. There was an expectation in the house, which Mother could not explain to me. But his return was not particularly joyful. He brought me a sackful of toys, but there was no light in his face. Later I understood that the meeting had been a disappointment.

Now I saw the *Ostjuden* for the first time: short, thin, standing next to the kiosk and guzzling. Some of them were still dressed in the old style. They seemed chained to each other, even while eating. There was no glory in their nocturnal appearance. Except for Theresa, who kept her dreamy gaze fixed on them, they would have escaped my notice this time too.

"Where are they going?" she asked again.

"I don't know," said Mother.

The darkness descended now from the high, riddled roofs and the suspended tanks. People crowded together on the third-class platforms. The first-class platform was empty. Father stood at the barrier as if he were keeping guard.

The express arrived and Theresa rose to her feet like a young girl still obedient to her parents' wishes. Father took the two colored suitcases and shoved them in. The coach was empty. The familiar scents of perfume and tobacco gave me a comfortable, domestic feeling. The mostly empty first-class coaches always greeted us with a green light because of the green curtains: a poor reflection, but still palpable, of the forests and parks we had left behind us. The few, scattered faces always seemed to me veiled or ill, but not lacking in sharpness. For hours on end I would watch the silently bouncing landscape, enchanted by the soundless music rising into the air.

Now for some reason the coach looked impoverished. Maybe because the curtains were brown. The corners were full of shadows, the abandoned shadows of people who had been here a few hours before.

While the coach glided through the darkness and the first-class passengers were served midnight coffee, Theresa awoke from her waking sleep and said, "I'm not going back to the sanatorium." Her soft face was dark and sullen and her mouth a sharp, resolute line.

"What are you talking about?" said Mother insincerely. "We never dreamed of it. . . ."

"In that case, swear to me."

"I swear."

Now it was clear that words were of no avail. Again she demanded that we take her home, not to our house, but to her parents.

"But we have no parents any more," said Mother imploringly.

Theresa's answer was cruel. "Of course we haven't; we killed them." Her voice trembled with an accusing pathos, as if she were talking not about herself but about some moral wrong that had been done to her. As the train rushed on, she rose to her feet and announced that we would get off at the next station. She couldn't stand the green smells and the evil plots being hatched

around her. Mother pleaded with her, swore that nobody meant her any harm. There was no one in the
compartment but us. But Theresa did not seem to hear.
At the first station, we got off, dragging our suitcases
like poor people.

It was already almost midnight. The sound of cold
water murmured in the empty station. The signals
flashed and the train slipped away into the night. It
transpired that the little troop of Jews with their bundles
also alighted here. With their little children screaming
they looked like a parcel that had come apart.

"Where are we?" asked Theresa angrily.

"I don't know," said Father.

Strangely enough, Father's wrath was now directed
toward the wretched little band of wanderers—as
though they were following us with malicious intent.
Theresa and her illness were forgotten. The two colored
suitcases, the glory of the holiday, lay despised on the
ground.

"You see them wherever you go," said Father in a
furious voice.

Mother kept trying to pacify Theresa with all kinds
of words whose meaning I could not understand. In the
end she admitted that they really had intended taking
Theresa back to the sanatorium, and said that she was
now very sorry for it.

But Theresa's eyes were full of dark suspicion. Distant church bells chimed midnight and we stood in the
gateway next to the locked warehouses, with the
wretched band of wanderers whom the station guard
would not allow to enter. Together we stood under the
chilly night sky of the summer.

"Where shall we go?" Mother ventured to ask.

"We'll go to the church," said Theresa firmly.

"The churches are all closed at night."

"That makes no difference."

"Let's go anywhere, as long as we don't stay here,"
said Father, drawing himself up. The station guard
knew nothing, except that there were no more trains
that night.

"And is there a hotel anywhere near?"

"I think not."

"If there are no people here and no hotels, why does the express stop here?"

"He's asking me," said the guard.

"Who should I ask if not you?"

"You can ask me anything you like, just don't expect any answers."

"And a coach—is there no coach here either?"

"There's someone over there, sleeping on the bench."

The darkness spread in a dense circle around the few station lights. The summer chill, damp from the river, smacked our faces and stole into our coats.

The sleeping coachman agreed to take us. We sat shivering and huddled in the old coach, swaying over unpaved roads and narrow country bridges in the wake of Theresa's sick caprice.

"Don't listen to them. Drive to the church," Theresa instructed the coachman.

"Madam, the churches are closed at night. There's no one there."

"Drive to the church, I said."

"You're not the boss. If the boss wants to go to the church, I'll take you there."

"Drive to the church," said Father.

"Why didn't you say so in the first place? Now I'll have to turn back again," grumbled the coachman. Father too seemed hypnotized by Theresa's iron will. The coach climbed hill after hill. Lights came and went in the darkness, dim flickers beckoning in the misty distance. It seemed that the journey would never end.

At last the coach came to a stop next to a little country church surrounded by a plain picket fence.

"We're here. What now?" called the coachman, as if he were dealing not with people but with ghosts.

Father got out and stood there as if he no longer had a will of his own. Theresa grew taller in the darkness, like a feverish priestess. Mother stood bowed down by her side. As we waited to see what she would do, she began striding toward the gate, pushing aside fallen

branches as if she knew her way in the dark. We followed her blindly. She stood at the locked gate for a
moment and knelt, bowing her head in a gesture of de-
vout Christianity. She crossed herself and immediately
burst into strangled weeping that shook her whole body.

We bent down to lift her up into the coach.

"Go!" shouted Father furiously, as if he wanted to
give the horses wings. We were on a downward slope
and the horses galloped. Theresa howled and her body
shook. Mother wrapped her in the winter raincoat.

"Faster!" Father urged the coachman. But the horses
proceeded at their own pace without making any special effort. All the rest of that night we jogged along
dubious roads, between bushes and on hard ground.

When dawn broke we had reached the sleeping station. Pale shadows crossed Father's face, as if an alien
force had taken possession of him. Mother tried hard
to be practical. The coachman demanded a huge sum,
and Father shrugged and didn't even try to haggle.

Theresa fell asleep in Mother's arms.

We climbed down slowly into the first, faint light.
Did the express stop here? The station master, who
was already sitting in his place, said that sometimes it
stopped and sometimes it didn't. It had its instructions
from the center.

"And you have nothing to say in the matter?"

"No."

Father stood next to the two colored suitcases looking as if he were about to give way to his despair.

The express came on time and stopped.

We carried Theresa into the nearly empty first-class
carriage. Her sleep was deep, bound up with the wanderings of the night. The pale shadows clung to Father's
face, sucking the marrow from his bones.

I remembered how cheerful the journey home from
Baden used to be. And now we were prisoners even in
our own familiar express, passing painfully through the
old familiar places. Two ladies slowly sipped their
morning coffee. Their elderly faces expressed a hor-
rible satisfaction. It was as if they were part of our

nightmare. In the next compartment the conductor
struggled with a violent drunk. The drunk cursed the
Jews and their money and the trains that never came
on time. The conductor took no notice of his cursing,
but simply asked him to step aside. The two old ladies
stopped talking and looked at us out of the corners of
their eyes, not with any direct intention, but watchfully.
The light spread and the familiar forests and pastures
that we had crossed year after year ever since my early
childhood were revealed once more in the first radiance
of morning. The frown on Theresa's forehead melted
and its pallor was pure. Now I knew: Theresa never
had been spoken of openly in our house, only in words
suggestive of some religious mystery—or of premature
death.

The train rushed on and the fear that soon we would
have to confront Theresa again crept into our thoughts.
But Theresa's sleep had evidently done her good. She
woke up and her face shone with the gentleness of ac-
ceptance. She did not ask where we were going or why,
as if she had agreed of her own free will to return to
the sanatorium. And this immediately made us feel
uneasy, as if we had deceived her.

Mother asked, "Don't you want to come home with
us?"

"The holiday is over." Theresa smiled. "The sisters
are expecting me." Now she spoke of the sisters as
kindred souls or blood relatives. Mother asked, for
some reason, if she needed a coat, and Theresa said
that everything at the sanatorium was wonderfully well
organized. The nuns prayed in the morning, and anyone who wanted could join in. Meals were served on
time. She spoke slowly, with the meekness of her
thoughts dominated by the tranquil sanatorium. But our
relief was accompanied by a sensation of being suddenly rendered superfluous, cast out of her illness.

The end of the journey approached. We reached the
sanatorium at noon. Bewildered, we stood in the vaulted
space with its concrete religious symbols. It was a

convent named after St. Peter with a sanatorium in its courtyard. The nuns greeted us in friendly fashion and asked no questions.

Theresa was now brisk, polite, and hospitable, like a woman returning to her own home and familiar furnishings: to me it seemed that she would soon remove her holiday clothes and don a nun's habit. Mother's face was all squeezed up, as though she were going to cry. But she didn't. Her hands were stretched out awkwardly in front of her, as if they were ashamed of having nothing to do.

Thus we found ourselves suddenly dispossessed of our obligations, all alone in that tranquil space of ample lawns, statues, and fountains. Two of the nuns embraced Theresa gently, and there was nothing for us to do but watch her walk away from us over the white marble floor. I noted: Theresa did not embrace Mother.

It was night when we reached home. The two colored suitcases stood in the corner of the hall. All the humiliations of the journey had been absorbed into their leather. Father put on slippers and regained his composure. The rooms were untidy, as if strangers had been on a spree here in our absence. Mother did not take off her dress. She sat in an armchair, her big eyes blurred with faded makeup. I sat huddled on the sofa, hoping that someone would come and take off my shoes. But Mother did not approach me. A cold, consuming sadness rose from every corner of the room.

Later on, Mother and Father sat by the table in the corner and ate sardines out of a tin. They dipped their bread in the oil and ate without a word. It seemed to me that never before had they eaten like this, with such mechanical movements. Their hunger had apparently driven all their former habits from them.

I tried to remember, but there was nothing that haunted my memory, save the icon in the convent waiting room of Mary with a pink baby at her breast, this pinkness, on a dark field, that spread and dripped into my brain.

6

SUDDENLY the rain poured down. One of Father's unknown enemies began publishing a series of articles denouncing his work. The remote provincial paper, which usually dealt with local politics, economics, and features for women, had found a sensational new topic—my father's books. "A man never knows where his enemies are hiding," said Father when he came across the first copy of the paper. From the opening article it was apparent that the enemy wanted more than to wound: he was out for a kill.

To his first question, who are the author's heroes, he replied: neither urban Austrians nor rural Austrians, but Jews, who had lost all semblance of humanity and were now useless, corrupt, perverted; parasites living off the healthy Austrian tradition, not their own marrow but the marrow of others. It could not be denied that this parasitism possessed a certain beauty, but it was a parasitic beauty.

The article was cruel and vicious, but it still left room for some kind of merit, especially when it enlarged on the subject of the unhealthy beauty of the parasite. Father was indignant but tried to hide it. He thought that one of his many friends would come to his defense. But not one did. A week passed, and the second article appeared. This time the accusation was open. The object of the attack was not the writing but the writer. The critic had gone to the trouble of digging up obscure early works in order to show how the parasitism had taken root and form, how it had penetrated the very pith of Austrian art, and how on this soil it produced its spores. Here were no human beings with warm-blooded human feelings pulsing in their veins, but insubstantial wraiths with cold, evil intellects. As proof he adduced everything from great to small, even poems Father had written in his youth for the student magazine.

We couldn't even argue that the articles were written by an anti-Semite. The critic, as his name showed, was a Jew. Week after week the articles came out and nobody bothered to reply. As if everyone agreed with their damning judgements. A hard autumn descended on the town and Father went down to the coal cellar and brought up two pails full. Mother put up the double windows. And friends who dropped in of an evening spoke, of course, about the vicious, slanderous articles covering whole pages in the paper and blackening Father's name. Father maintained his composure, but his face showed that it wasn't easy.

At the same time Theresa's first letters began arriving from the convent. She wrote of the devoted care of the nuns and of the quiet enveloping the plants growing in the gardens. Long, detailed letters permeated with the serenity of the convent, and a kind of clarity that made you think of bracing winter air.

With not a trace of anger or complaint, as though her life had anchored in a warm harbor, she wrote about her daily routine: getting up in the morning, breakfast, a walk, the well-stocked library. Supper was served in the old building; the evening ended with a prayer. Mother read and wept.

For the first time the new words appeared: contemplation, the ladder of prayer, meditation, and purification. And other words too, whose meaning I did not understand but which I sensed as subtle, whispering words you were not allowed to speak out loud.

Mother packed clothes separately, sweets and chocolates separately, a jar of preserves and some cheese straws. Even though she didn't say, "They're for

Theresa," I knew. I went with her to the post office. It was a long walk down the length of Hapsburg Avenue. Mother said nothing and I listened to the rhythm of her footsteps. Nothing in my daily routine had changed. German, Latin, and algebra, and in the afternoons, learning passages by heart.

The venomous articles began to take their toll. Father would read them again and again. We could hear him wrestling with his absent enemy, grinding his teeth; only the evenings made him forget his shame. In the evenings friends would come and fill the house with noise. Father repeatedly declared he was preparing a detailed reply that would expose the scoundrel in his true colors: "the scoundrel" was now our name for the obscure critic from the provinces.

But in the meantime the scoundrel had escaped the pages of the newspapers and invaded the house itself; not a corner was free of his presence. From week to week the articles grew longer, proclaiming from one end of Austria to the other: the Jewish parasite must be rooted out.

But no man knows his time. The articles were still coming out, their voice loud all over the land, when the obscure critic died. The editor of the newspaper eulogized him on the middle page. And now for the first time we learned that he had been a very sick man, bedridden, and that his last articles had been written with the help of his sister. A strange feeling of relief descended on the house. Father was not happy though: all he said was, "No man knows his time, or his place either." The evil spirits went on haunting the house, but their power was waning. From time to time we still heard Father cursing through clenched teeth. But gradually he fell silent and returned to his books.

Theresa's letters now came one after the other. Father would read them and exclaim over the accuracy of her descriptions and the richness of her emotions. It was clear she was enchanted by the life of the convent, and it was not only the beauty of the landscape to which her senses were opening. Her writing was clear and delicate, with no smudges or crossing out. We shut ourselves up with Theresa's letters, reading passages aloud, or simply standing, looking out of the window.

One morning Mother stood up and said, "I'm going."

"Where to?"

"St. Peter's."

She came home in the evening, wrapped in a woollen shawl, her face flushed and her brow expressionless. Her former sorrow had stiffened on her lips and become alien and static. To Father's questions she replied that Theresa was well-dressed, her room was tidy, and that apart from the New Testament her table was bare. She spoke freely about everything. I noticed that Mother's choice of words was very balanced. She spoke quietly and without going into superfluous details. Father asked if Theresa was really considering conversion, and what the procedure would be, and Mother replied that the subject had not been discussed at all.

The days grew more and more silent. The obscure critic was transformed. No longer the scoundrel, but Taucher, Michael Taucher in full. And Taucher, moreover, the perceptive, Taucher the discriminating. Poor Taucher who died young, Taucher whose poor sister had to look after him . . . and thus Taucher settled down and took up residence amongst us as an adopted member of the family.

And when Mother tried to refute one of the obscure critic's contentions, Father would say indignantly, "I don't know what you're talking about. Can't you see that he bases everything on the texts themselves?" Or sometimes he would burst out angrily, "You don't understand!" And all the time, between my Latin and algebra lessons and the passages from old German literature I had to learn by heart, that clever comedian roamed around the house, rolling from room to room in his wheelchair. There was no need to ask him any questions. Everything had already been answered. All we had to do was read his articles. Mother tried to comfort Father with home-baked delicacies. Father put on weight and his face sank into his neck.

7

THE last long vacation we spent with Aunt Gusta at her cottage in the country. By then it was clear that the sunlight was no longer ours, nor the trees. Nevertheless, there was still a communion between us and the few austere objects that Aunt Gusta cherished so lovingly.

Aunt Gusta lay limply with her eyes open, the medicine tray on the low straw chair a bitter emblem of her prolonged illness. The long hours infused with the mixed odors from one bout of baking to the next merged until, before we knew it, evening was upon us, filling us with the sudden fear of an approaching end.

Father was reading the proofs of his new book. He absorbed himself in the work of the final corrections with a grim frenzy, like a man on whom fortune no longer smiled. He tore many pages out of his new book. Telegrams and express letters upset the quiet of the country cottage almost every day. The publisher was apparently at a loss to understand the passion for cutting that had overcome the writer. He pleaded and threatened, and flooded us with urgent letters.

The month of June passed in this strange urgency. In the end Father resigned himself to all the imperfections. He wrote a long, apologetic introduction and recovered his spirits. And the days that came afterward were peaceful, breathing with the slow rhythm of the countryside. Father wore his country shorts and Mother worked in the garden, her face veiled in a transparent scarf. The water in the stream flowed in mute abundance, as if it wanted to drown the din of the impatient days in its quiet welling. And right away came the walks: short at first, then branching out into a shady forest of dumb silences and subdued footsteps. Even Aunt Gusta recovered. God forbid that anyone should mention Vienna, Prague, newspapers, or literary journals. A marvellous forgetfulness came with the scents of the blossoming trees, casting us into a dense, shadowy thicket. And the days merged secretly with the nights. The early wakings, the long walks, the closeness beyond words that brought us back in the evenings sunburned and tired, moved in time to some blind melody.

In the month of July heavy rains fell, and we were obliged to stay indoors. Father remembered his flawed work and his face darkened with sorrow. Mother tried to distract him, but in vain. Each defect came and stood before him, demanding its revenge. We knew: invisible thorns were sticking in his flesh.

Doctor Mirzel appeared. In the summer he stayed with his aged mother and in winter he went back to Vienna. He was then writing his well-known work, "The Destruction of Judaism—Relief and Recovery." Father had known him since he was a boy: they had studied together in Vienna and for a time they had been together in Prague. Mother thought it best to surround Father with people and not to leave him alone. But Mirzel did not bring relief and distraction. He would come, nibble cake, drink coffee, and spread his cheerful despair at the top of his voice. The argument would become one-sided: Mirzel with himself. His animosity was colorful, full of wit and power—a deep well from which he drew up words, proverbs, jokes, and even snatches of song. Father withdrew into himself. The many defects he had discovered in his latest work had broken his spirit, although he maintained a façade of his old ways. Nobody knew what was happening behind his mute mask. And the summer rains, which had once made us lighthearted, shut us up together in crowded intimacy. Of me nothing was demanded any more, neither Latin nor mathematics, nor even practicing the violin. I read Karl May, and in the evenings Mother would come and sit with me for hours. Light and silence would advance side by side across the warm borders of sleep. When Mother said, "I don't understand," it meant that something had happened. But whatever it was was beyond my comprehension. Mirzel's gaiety frightened me. And in the morning I would stand next to the window and measure the circles of light crowding against the window screens.

But Mother thought it necessary to keep Father entertained, whether by an evening's gossip or by Dr. Mirzel's gay despair. The rain did not cease, and the stony silence between Dr. Mirzel's comings and goings weighed heavily on us. Since he was our only visitor, the words he left behind echoed harshly in the empty house: the Jews had no talent for art. All they were capable of producing were cantors and comedians. Although they filled the journals and boulevard theaters, the contribution of the Jews to Austrian culture should not be exaggerated. They had a place, perhaps, in light comedy. . . . Were these remarks directed against Father? It was hard to say. Father did not write comedies, but he certainly wrote for journals. His novels sold well and he was popular in Vienna and Prague. But this last year an ugly, orange fog had begun to cloud his eyes—a taut discontent that left its traces on his face. He suffered from frequent dizzy spells. His dormant ulcer woke and began troubling him. He would sit in his armchair for hours on end like a man listening to secret disease spread through his body. The hope that the vacation, the grandeur of the scenery, would distract him a little—this hope did not last long. Mother complained about the rain that kept us stuck indoors.

At the end of July Uncle Lumpel and his young wife, Sirell, arrived unexpectedly. Uncle Lumpel could think of nothing but his business affairs. These prospered, but not on as large a scale as he would have liked. Aunt Sirell's interests were confined to fashion and cosmetics.

As always, they arrived in a flurry of urban uproar. Of course they had lost their suitcases at the station, but in the end they had recovered them with no harm done. Aunt Sirell, as usual, told the whole story in exhausting detail. She sighed affectedly, blamed her husband, and swooned into an armchair. We were always put off balance by her arrival. But Mother still thought it for the best to keep Father surrounded by people and not to leave him alone. Aunt Sirell recovered, complained bitterly, laughed, and then burst into tears. The world around her was nothing more than a constant stimulus to her own self-indulgence. Father sank deeper into depression.

The weather improved suddenly and saved us. We ate lunch on a rustic cloth spread on the grass. The ugly orange cloud lifted from Father's eyes. He imitated Sirell's pouts and Dr. Mirzel's gesticulations. Long walks brought the soft expression back to his face. Our old words seemed to come alive again. We were wrapped up in each other like children.

But for the evenings things would have been better. Uncle Lumpel and Aunt Sirell settled down comfortably as if they were in a middle-class hotel. They opened their suitcases and spread their clothes about; and the heavy perfume and faint smell of mothballs stripped the house of its monastic austerity.

Uncle Lumpel's arrogance, the arrogance of a prosperous businessman, was more overbearing than usual, perhaps because he had succeeded in setting up a branch in Salzburg. He never tired of attacking modern literature: it was a swindle and a cheat, obsessed by bad dreams because of its own bad conscience. He was referring, of course, to Kafka, whom Father revered as a prophet of truth.

Father could not restrain himself and the arguments began. Old, obscure affairs, incomprehensible to me, were dragged up in ugly and acrimonious detail, including the inheritance, of course, which a few months before had been divided by the court after prolonged quarrels and litigation.

Father denounced the Jewish petite bourgeoisie, for whom the world consisted of nothing but money, hotels, and holiday resorts, and a stupid, superficial religion. Uncle Lumpel gave back as good as he got, denouncing modern literature that conjured wraiths and nightmares and sexual perversions out of its own morbid imagination. Father shouted, "Jewish entrepreneurs should be wiped off the face of the earth, they ruin everything they touch!" The next day they left as though the house were on fire.

Ugly, tormented spirits settled on the house. Father did not write, correct proofs, or reply to the many letters piling up on his desk; and if anyone mentioned one of his books, he twisted his face into a bitter grimace. Aunt Gusta's health deteriorated. The old country doctor spread his hands and said a doctor would have to be fetched from town, the sooner the better. This loyal old man, who regarded himself as a Jew because of his grandfather, a Jewish doctor who had converted to Christianity, grew very close to us during Gusta's illness, and asked many questions about Jewish customs. And then came the hopeless, desperate running around: doctors were summoned one after the other, from the provincial capital and from Vienna. Father would come back from town tired, broken, and sometimes drunk. Mother would sit beside him as if he were ill. Aunt Gusta was dying slowly, day by day, in full consciousness. The frantic trips from the village to the provincial capital, the doctors and the drugs, the constant presence of the old country doctor who clung to us like a brother, did nothing to relieve Father's anguish. We knew: between one waiting room and the next he spent his time sitting in bars or gambling on the roulette wheel. Mother's grief was self-contained.

My own little life seemed to have gone astray in the commotion. The shadows of the forest merged into the full splendor of the summer's end. From the front window I could see the patchwork of fields stretching flat to the horizon. The thought that all this calm beauty was doomed quivered in me, a naked fear.

But for the express letters things would have been easier. The letters were a constant reminder of the demands of the outside world: publishers, journals, articles that Father had promised to write. The long summer evenings, once a source of modest domesticity, were now brightly lit and shadowless, like a sleepless hospital: Mother in a slack dressing gown, the doctors in Aunt Gusta's room, Father dozing like a blind messenger who had played his part and now could only sink into an armchair. The old doctor no longer interfered, as if the subjects now being discussed in the sickroom were beyond his comprehension.

Among the letters were also a few postcards and family invitations, which in other circumstances would have aroused little interest. Uncle Frum had converted and gone to study theology in Antwerp; a well-known cousin of ours had written an attack on Judaism as a religion without divine grace. These were our family's hidden wounds, now being exposed one after the other like secrets that could no longer be kept.

Father did not protest, but only said, "The strong go out to greet life confidently." I knew that many things lay hidden in this sentence. In particular I took note of the word "confidently," which Uncle Lumpel was fond of using.

The old doctor, Dr. Meister, now announced, "I have never been ashamed of my Jewish origins." He spoke in all innocence, but Father, for some reason, thought that the old doctor was trying to console him and said, "Speaking for myself, I have nothing to boast about. My Jewishness means nothing to me."

That night the doctors never left the sickroom. The whispered words reaching our ears were faint and unintelligible, as if they came from another world. In the early hours of the morning the doctors emerged from her room, the verdict sealed on their faces.

At the end of the week Aunt Gusta died, and we were left with the task of burying her according to the customs of her forefathers, which she had written down in a notebook before she died. Father brought some

Jews from the provincial capital. They spoke in an unintelligible language and scurried about the rooms kicking up a racket. It was ugly and shameful, but since it was her last wish we did everything mutely and submissively. It was strange to see Father standing there with a shabby felt hat on his head.

And when we came back from the funeral the rooms seemed violated. The clear light trembled convulsively on the walls. The crumpled curtains looked distorted. No one went to close the shutters. In the evening Dr. Meister came and sat on a low chair like a supplicant. No one tried to make him feel at home and his humble air added to our shame.

The next day Father did not go to the provincial capital. Mother tried to restore the monastic calm to the rooms, but she couldn't stop the wild summer light from breaking in.

That evening we read the will. It was written in a pedantic hand and plain language. She asked our forgiveness but did not make the customary references to God. For three days the wax candles burned on the sideboard and on the fourth day they went out. The darkness of evening descended on the cottage.

Low, meaningless days chained us together. Father drank, tore up manuscripts, cursed his publishers and his own writing that never amounted to anything. Mother stood like the accused at a court-martial.

And thus our last long holiday came to an end.

It was the summer of 1938. I was twelve years old and Father was forty-three. Nobody knew what the future held in store and what experiences awaited us.

We left the cottage in haste, as if we were expected at another funeral elsewhere. At the station the train was waiting where we had left it, the bottom edges of its coaches grimy with soot. In the kiosk, workers were drinking their morning coffee. An elegantly dressed woman stood apart, scornfully watching the anxious haste of a family shepherding many small children. A thin drizzle was falling. There was no friend to see us off, only strangeness everywhere. And we too, Father and Mother and I, seemed bereft of affection and of words. Father pushed the green suitcase inside with a grim expression on his face, like a day laborer.

When we came home the summer light was weak and cold. Mother put on a zippered green dressing gown, and her face hovering above the shabby old garment expressed an unnatural composure.

Mother said, "I didn't tell Aunt Gusta anything about Theresa. I'm glad I didn't tell her."

"Didn't she ask?" Father inquired.

"She did ask and I said that everything was fine. Don't you think I was right?"

Father's face was swollen about the jaws again. I sensed some new discontent brewing in him.

Mother said, "I didn't want to burden her."

The thought that the country cottage with its monastic austerity now stood shut up and empty, with the plants dying in the garden, and that when the old country doctor walked past the gate he bowed his head piously, these thoughts touched a mute chord inside me and made it tremble.

Father broke this delicate mood with the following remark: "I hate the Jewish petite bourgeoisie." I knew: he was referring to Uncle Lumpel and Aunt Sirell, who had flooded us with their vulgar commotion.

Theresa's letters grew fewer. She no longer said anything about herself, only about the convent and its way of life. From the few hints she dropped we learned that some of the secrets of its mystery had already been revealed to her and that she was struggling to fathom the rest. The way she addressed us was colder now and lacking in tender touches, except for the signature: your loving sister Theresa. Father still exclaimed over the accuracy of her descriptions, her choice of adjectives, and her ability to write in a language so simple and precise.

Father returned to his desk and I to my lessons. Now it was history: two compositions to write. The Committee for the Advancement of Literature decided to hold its meetings in our house. The Committee was very correct, and well known for the impartiality of its judgements. At the last meeting there was a difference of opinion; Father threatened to resign, and the members of the Committee decided to postpone the final decision to a later date.

Mother put on winter clothes to go visit Theresa. She looked strange in her winter clothing. The heavy garments made her clumsy. It seemed to me that the bitter secret, the secret she had not told Aunt Gusta, still oppressed her, although she kept on repeating that she was glad she had not told Aunt Gusta anything. It was a damp, ugly evening and Mother set out on her journey from the back door.

8

I REMEMBER the evening light, pure and solid, resting on the double windows, the stove full of embers; but more than these I remember the bundle of shadows the young woman brought with her and deposited on the floor like long, fragile objects: and also the wicker basket she brought, with the baby in it.

The woman sat in an armchair and the shadows she had brought with her, the first shadows of frost, breathed by her side as if they feared to part from her. She looked to me then, in the delicate evening light, beautiful, as if she had walked out of one of the books I was reading. The rustic carpet suited her feet and her hands resting on her knees were relaxed and pensive. The baby did not cry. Her green eyes darted about in their narrow sockets. The woman sat gathered into her body, her head still and composed. The evening light lingered on her round face for a while, and then gradually darkened.

And when Father came home the lights were already on. The shadows the woman had brought with her were folded up in the dark corners. The baby closed her eyes and fell asleep. Father was glad, and I did not understand at first the meaning of the joy that came over his face. It appeared that she came from the village, the village where Father was born. "I can't believe it, I can't believe it," cried Father. As if a life he never expected to see again had returned to him.

And when he recovered he asked, "Are there still

people there?" The young woman raised her face to him and it was full of wondering attention. Father asked if the trees next to the post office were still standing. She hung her head shyly.

Father talked and talked. Mother shrank from the words Father brought up out of his memory. There was a winter smell about the sounds, as if they had come to us with sleigh bells attached to them. In the end she too opened her mouth and said, "The river came up wild. The bridge nearly collapsed." They spoke until late at night. The pauses between the sentences grew longer. And I fell asleep on the bench in the silences between the words.

When I woke, the autumn light had already crossed the passage. The stove was roaring. And the smell of milk spread through the house, now full of a sudden joy. In the morning light I saw: the wondering look still suffused the woman's face, and even when she took care of her baby's needs the look did not go away. She did not ask me, like other women, how old are you? She only wrapped me in a look as soft as down.

"And do they still remember me?" asked Father.

"They remember." A narrow slit opened in her closed mouth.

About Father's native village I had heard a little in my very early childhood. But for the last two years, and maybe even before that, Father had stopped talking about it. Sometimes the happy memory of the village would gush up in me and I would ask him to tell me about it. But Father would ignore my request and make up some other story for me. Mother would take my hand in hers, and this was as enjoyable as the story itself. Even then the evenings were clearer than the mornings. Perhaps because words spoken at night, before sleep comes, partake of the nature of sleep and fall like seeds into the receptive earth.

From her few remarks I understood: she had been on the road for weeks. Her fiancé had broken his promises, she had received some letters from him but without a proper address. Country people never change: the

Jewish families had dwindled, most of them were old now, but they were still ruled by the old beliefs. Strange, she showed no signs of anger, no fear or expression of emotion. Neither tears nor laughter, but only a kind of wonder. And the questions Father asked now seemed full of wonder too. I closed my eyes and saw a village: a few old men standing at the windows, angry with their children who had abandoned them, their bitter anger pouring out of their eyes like a thick liquid.

Father returned to his usual affairs and involvements: the Jewish–Christian League was about to expand its journal and wanted to appoint him editor. The first edition would, of course, be devoted to Martin Buber. Martin Buber was a household word amongst us. Some of Father's friends spoke of him with veneration and compared him to one of the ancient apostles. Others cast doubt on his gospel. The arguments were sometimes stormy. Father's attitude was very difficult for me to gauge. Once he too had admired Buber, but his admiration was no longer wholehearted. Nowadays he admired nothing. His enthusiasm had waned, and a skeptical kind of smile played about his lips. Only Kafka, he was the only one Father spoke of in lowered tones, as of a true prophet. But who knew Kafka? Only very few. People didn't like black prophecies.

And thus, among all these grave questions and important matters Yetti took up her place, with her baby in her basket. As if she did not belong to our world but only to her own abandonment, to which she was reconciled. No one asked her what she was going to do or where she was going to turn in her darkness. Her calamity brought a strange kind of light into our house. Perhaps it was because of the baby, which was pink and healthy.

At that time Father was suing two journals. One had called him a Jewish writer sowing anxiety and glorifying weakness. The reason, of course, was that alien blood, not noble Austrian blood, flowed in his veins. The second journal called him a Jew in love with decadence. The journals refused to apologize. At first it seemed that the Jewish–Christian League would support him, but some of its leading members thought that there was no point rewarming this old dish. The evil would blow over of its own accord. Alone Father set out to engage his enemies in battle.

And in the evenings the raven, Dr. Mirzel, came and sat in our house, as usual. He made sarcastic jokes and called Father an incurably Jewish writer.

"Be so good as to tell me: what, precisely, is Jewish about my writing?"

"The anxiety. Isn't that a legacy inherited from former generations?"

"Isn't it rather a human trait? Are we animals?"

"Yes," said Dr. Mirzel slyly, "but it's foreign to Austrians, you must admit."

"I deny," thundered Father, "the Judaism others attribute to me."

"I understand," said Dr. Mirzel with open skepticism.

And so it went almost every evening until the end.

And only late at night, when I was already in bed, listening and not listening, Father, Mother, and Yetti would sit and talk about the remote, godforsaken village, Father's painful crucible. The longings penetrated my light sleep. Secret, intimate longings, like rain at night.

And one night she disclosed, as if by chance, that the deceitful lover was a Jew, a travelling salesman. Father was indignant. "What can you expect from those Jews? They should be rooted out." A strange gleam, like a hunter's, glinted in his eyes. I saw: Yetti's calamity had now taken on a terrible momentum in Father's eyes. He swore that he would bring the deceiver in chains to justice and have him disgraced. Yetti lowered her eyes as if it had nothing to do with her.

In this battle Father found many allies: a retired judge, a lawyer, the pharmacist, and a few businessmen whose affairs were in the doldrums. Even then it was obvious that the chances of finding the man were very slim, but Father did not give up. His anger was stronger than he.

At night two lawyers came to collect evidence. Yetti
told them about the village, the way of life there, and
the Jewish salesman who had promised her the world.
Strange, there was no bitterness in her voice. Her state-
ments were short and few. Afterward they would sit
and drink and denounce travelling salesmen and ped-
lars. Faceless Jews, cheating the rural population.

Evening after evening they came and questioned
her. Her memory was not very good. "I don't know,
I didn't ask. I was too shy. I believed him"—that was
all she could say. She blushed and her hands lay on her
knees in apathy.

On Yetti's face signs of a hidden happiness appeared
and grew. Perhaps it only seemed so, because of the
smile at the corners of her mouth. Perhaps she knew
that the search would uncover nothing. Or perhaps she
said to herself, "I don't want him any more." In any
case she did not condemn him, even when it seemed
expected of her.

Rain fell and Father began talking about the village
again. But without sentiment this time, with a bitter,
pitiless smile. Late at night Dr. Mirzel would come
and bring with him the outside cold and his resounding
voice. Once more the familiar, sarcastic drone: there's
nothing to be ashamed of. The Jewish Order isn't the
worst order, after all. Believe me, there are worse
orders to belong to.

I noticed: Yetti's face lost its embarrassment. A
youthful down grew on her cheeks. The people who
came to our house could not take their eyes off her.
They sought her out with a kind of lust. Yetti escaped
to the kitchen, as if seeking Mother's protection, but
here too they pursued her on various pretexts.

"Yetti," Father would call, "show your face."

And Yetti would come like a woman at her master's
beck and call.

Sometimes, when the house was full of a gay despair,
Father would embrace Yetti and say, "This is what the
girls in my village were like. Isn't she a sight for sore
eyes?"

And Mother would be overcome with embarrassment; and when she was embarrassed, deep lines ran down her chin. Yetti would sit in an armchair brighteyed with the enjoyment of a country girl being petted.

Our visitors no longer discussed important, abstract matters or Father's lawsuits. They drank and laughed, and their laughter, loud laughter, gave me a disagreeable, shameful sensation.

And so it went, every evening. Strange men and strange women. And apparently all because of Yetti. Words drifting on tobacco smoke and alcohol fumes vied with each other. "Forget your fiancé, there are better men than him over here." Yetti's disaster was turning into a strange celebration. She wore Mother's dresses and reeked of eau de cologne.

When the celebrants went home and the house was empty Mother sat in the armchair, spread the newspaper, and buried herself in it.

"Why don't you go to bed?" I heard Father's voice.

"I'm sitting here," said Mother.

The shadows Yetti had brought with her now ran wild. Music played ceaselessly. Father had changed: a nervous tic jumped wildly on his face. And I felt as if I had vanished from my own field of vision.

And between one cup of coffee and the next I remembered: how pure and simple Yetti had been when she arrived at our house, as if she had come simply to bring us a breath of fresh air from Father's native village. But everything had been turned upside down. Everyone was kind to Yetti. I understood: it was a strange kindness, a kindness with its own motives. Mother wept, and her weeping seeped into my sleep like a cold drizzle.

And Yetti, did she know what was going on around her? Her vocabulary did not grow. She continued speaking a country dialect and her two hands lay on her knees like those of a woman without guile: and nevertheless the nights were transformed into wild parties with light music and cigarette smoke filling the salon. I would be sent off to bed at an early hour, and this ignominious expulsion kept me awake for hours.

Our financial situation worsened. Mother thought we should stop inviting people to the house. Father shouted, "As long as I'm alive our house will be open to my friends. I don't live for myself alone."

The baby sickened, and the family doctor was in attendance day and night. Strange—Yetti ignored her cries now. Mother took care of the baby, but only grudgingly. And angry words, such as I had never heard in our house before, rent the air between laughter and laughter, like the cawing of crows.

For a few days the evil storm raged. The tic jumped wildly on Father's forehead. He was trapped in a gaiety not his own. Mother was busy tending the sick baby; and Yetti served coffee like a glamour girl.

One evening Mother burst in, the baby in her arms, and cried bitterly, "I won't permit this!"

"I don't live for myself alone," Father silenced her.

"There's a child in the house. As long as there's a child in the house, I can't permit this."

"But I permit it."

"I want you all to know," shouted Mother, "our money is finished. We are living on our debts."

Father stood up, his shame exposed to all eyes. Strange, no one went up to say good-bye or to console him. They all put on their winter coats and escaped from the house.

The next day Yetti put on her country shawl, took her baby in her arms, and said that she was going out for a breath of fresh air. It was a fine evening with a pink sky, like when she came only colder. No one imagined that she was leaving for good. The light changed and darkness suddenly descended.

Father came home late from a committee meeting, and ran to the station. He missed the train by a few minutes. It was the train on which Yetti had left. When he came home in the small hours of the night he said nothing. His body reeked of alcohol, and he looked pale and exhausted.

He slept for a whole day. Mother stood in the shadow of his sleep, fragile and despised, folding sheets and towels. The smell of milk that had warmed our house for a few weeks soured and exuded bitterness. A threatening orange fog settled on the windows and stayed there all day long. I didn't dare go into Father's room, as if there were doctors there.

The next day a bright light invaded the rooms, stripping the furniture of its shadows. In the stove a single ember guttered. Mother was wearing her green dressing gown. Her face was pale. Father was standing by the window.

"I didn't mean it," said Mother, trying to pin her voice onto the silence. Father turned his head and swept the room with his gaze. Later, morning coffee was served. Father's eyes did not move from the window. Mother shrank, clutching the coffee cup with both hands. The light grew stronger and swept the remnants of shadows out of the corners, which stood white and naked, like immodestly exposed skin.

The nights were long, brightly lit, and empty. A sick bitterness pinched Father's lips. He became more and more entangled in his lawsuits until there seemed no way out. At night the fleeting memories of Yetti took on a menacing substantiality. She still seemed to be sitting there in the corner with her shadows.

In vain Mother tried to give our meals their old serenity. Intimations of orphanhood had fallen on everything, even the drapes. Charged, unspoken words floated in the air like hidden accusations. Mother's face too was infected with the same sick bitterness. One evening Father said, "What more do you want? You chased her away, didn't you?" Mother wept and Father did not try to comfort her. I knew: everything I had once known, my childhood too, was over.

Yellow stains from the leaking pipes appeared on the ceiling, and Mother did not call in a plumber. A faint smell of rot filled the rooms to suffocation. Each day Mother, for some reason, continued to plead, "Dinner's ready." But Father preferred to eat sandwiches, giving his meals a crude haste.

The old words were resurrected. Words from before Yetti's arrival. Two registered letters arrived with the reminder that the external battle was not yet over; and although Father was claiming damages for libel, it seemed that the accuser had become the accused. Perhaps because of his face, his unshaven cheeks, and the way he ran from room to room rummaging for documents.

The rooms emptied. The light rushed in, as if Yetti had taken our shadows away with her own. Father in the back room stood and studied his claim for damages as if it was not his claim but his guilt, for which he could never atone.

9

THE news of Aunt Theresa's death reached us at
night, almost by chance, and Mother automatically began packing the two colored suitcases; but immediately
she realized that there was no need for them. The
distance from our house to St. Peter's was not so great
to make a change of clothing necessary. "We're ready,"
said Mother, with an everyday kind of gesture, as if we
were setting out for afternoon tea at the Embroidered
Rose café. "I'll just have a look at the railway timetable," said Father, shocked into his old practicality.
The bitter tidings had taken us completely by surprise:
no wonder our bodies went on running according to
their accustomed rhythms.

Over the past few weeks Theresa's letters had
stopped coming, and her memory, dominating us from
afar, had faded. I no longer thought of her, but of the
tall poplars planted in the heart of the convent. Sometimes I would imagine that I was still standing in the
passageway looking at the dark picture with the pink
baby floating on its waves of darkness. But Theresa
herself I no longer saw. Her memory seemed to have
sunk into me and been assimilated. And even now,
when the bitter tidings came, her young face did not
beckon me. Only the poplar trees—as if she had been
metamorphosed into the trees.

Although we knew that there were no trains at that
hour we set out for the railway station. The sculptor
Stark, a friend of Father's youth, accompanied us. The

son of a Jewish mother, Stark was at this time tortured by cruel perplexities. He sought refuge from his distress in various odd places, and to us too he came—tall, strong, and bearded, the picture of fitness. But it was only a front. For the past year he had been wandering from one rabbi to another and one rabbinical court to the next. The rabbis did not welcome him. His robust, Aryan looks only made them suspicious. In the end one of the rabbis said to him, "Why take this trouble on yourself at a time like this?" They put him off on all kinds of pretexts, but their unwillingness only fuelled his obscure passion to return to the crucible of his origins, the origins of the mother he adored; it was her faith, or rather the faith of her forefathers, that he wanted to embrace.

Father was neither kind nor understanding, and even rebuked him. "What do you need it for, Kurt? And at a time like this. Believe me, Judaism has nothing to offer you, or me either. It simply doesn't exist. But for the anti-Semites it would have vanished long ago." Mother took no part in the discussion.

And thus, with everyone preoccupied by his own affairs, the bitter tidings reached us. Our house was a strange place that night, as if a thick fog had descended on it. Mother stood in the doorway, poorly dressed, wearing boots. Nor did Father's practical air seem appropriate to the occasion. His actions appeared to be prompted by deep confusion. Only the artist Stark seemed capable of rising to the occasion. With his two big, hairy hands he tried to shelter us.

We went to the station on foot. It did not occur to Father to hail a cab or take a shortcut. We walked the full length of Hapsburg Avenue. Mother walked in front. Father, for some reason, spoke about St. Peter's estates, where, as a young man, he had once secluded himself in the home of an enlightened aristocrat, an eccentric with liberal tendencies. It was there that he had first discovered the beauties of Austria's mountain country. But something in him had prevented him from sinking into that quiet beauty—it must have been the Jewish virus gnawing at him even then.

We did not speak about Theresa. It was as if she no longer belonged to the occasion. In the end Stark dared to ask if she had been in the convent for many years. And Father told him that at first she had been a patient in the hospital there, on account of her frequent depressions, but that in the course of time she had found a broader interest in the monastic way of life and in the theological study groups that took place there in the evenings.

"And what did you . . . ?" asked Stark hesitantly.

"She seems to have been happy," said Father.

Mother walked in front of us with a steady step. There was no one in the streets, only the autumn damp. We walked for a long time, and suddenly Father recovered his voice. He spoke about the still, dispassionate eye necessary to the artist, without which great art was impossible.

The mist thickened, and we arrived at the railway station. It was already after midnight. The damp emptiness glared from every corner. Two young women leaned silently on the counter of the kiosk. Their faces expressed a dark stupidity. Father approached the closed ticket booth, and when he saw that it was, in fact, closed, he turned to us. "We must make inquiries. There must be more trains. People and goods have to be transported, after all."

The conductor's answer was not long in coming: No trains. Only a local cattle train at dawn.

"Never mind," said Father. "We'll travel with the horses. We're not afraid of animals."

One of the guards standing at a distance made the following remark: "Austrian horses smell better than Jews."

For a moment there was silence. Mother's trembling hands stilled. The sculptor Stark pricked up his ears in the direction of the voice and called out, "Where are you, stranger? Why don't you show your face?"

"You'd better not provoke him," said the station master. "He's a violent man."

"We, at any rate," said Stark, "have not yet lost our humanity. We're prepared to fight."

"Words aren't worth fighting over," said the station master. "Leave him alone."

Strange—it was as if the reason for our coming here had been forgotten. It was after midnight and Mother suggested going for a walk, and maybe having a cup of coffee at the Embroidered Rose. Stark said that he himself was spoiling for a fight, but that the man was a coward, hiding in the dark. Stark's deep, full voice inspired us with confidence.

We went down the avenue and for a moment found ourselves standing in open fields covered with mist. Stark was huddled into his overcoat. Although we were already on the threshold of the Embroidered Rose, Mother kept insisting that the coffee there was strong and fresh and the cakes were homemade, and there was no better place to go to at this time of night. It wasn't her own voice, but a voice left over from other days.

The Embroidered Rose was open. A few scattered faces bent over the wooden tables, downing a midnight beer. They weren't drunk, but there was a heavy odor. Stark suddenly seemed full of high spirits and with a sweeping gesture, perhaps inappropriate to the occasion, turned to us and announced, "My friends, allow a half-breed to treat you."

"How much do you want for the Austrian mess of pottage?" said Father.

"The Austrian pound of flesh you can have for nothing."

"You'll live to regret the deal."

Father and Stark ordered cognac. Mother and I drank café au lait. The waitress stroked my head and said, "What a lovely boy. Nobody took me to cafés at night. Never mind. Life won't be a stranger to you."

"And you, my dear, when did you first go out into the night?" Father asked her mischievously.

"Very late. My parents were Catholics. They never let me out of the house."

"And how long did you submit to it?"

"Not very long, to tell the truth."

Stark did not join in the conversation. He was concentrating on the cognac. Suddenly I sensed with a kind of childish clarity the intimacy that existed between us and the artist Stark. As if he weren't a fleeting guest but a kindred soul of many years standing.

Mother watched us with a full, direct look. I could not read the expression in her eyes. A thin veil, transparent but impenetrable, now divided me from her. Her hands lay on the table, open and exposed.

I wondered again about this marvel called Stark, about his strange vicissitudes and the hidden passion which had driven him in recent years. And now he was sitting with us, waiting for the train to take us to Aunt Theresa's death. He never even knew her.

"Why take this trouble on yourself at a time like this?" My father's voice echoed in my ears. "It passes my understanding." Stark absorbed the voice and was silent. As for Father, he was driven by a different devil, a terrible devil: his writing. During the past year the literary journals had stopped counting him among the writers of Austria. Once they would allude to his Jewishness indirectly. Now they spoke openly about the alien elements, the germs of decadence, sown in all his sentences. Healthy people should keep away from his works. Father used to declare: "Freedom of expression above all. Without freedom of expression there is no room for thought." How many lawyers had earned their keep from his claims, lawsuits and appeals? . . . Now there was no more money to sustain them. Now Father ground his teeth and blamed himself, his writing, which had never amounted to anything because he had failed to learn from the French. Only they knew the right frame of mind, the quiet, unemotional detachment without which all writing was moralistic, or fantastical, or rootless. And he was thus ready to admit that neither he nor Wassermann nor Zweig nor even Schnitzler had attained any real standing in art. Strange—now that he had no more money left to sue the papers and journals for libel, he sat and accused himself. These accusations had a very bitter sound.

I had heard Stark say, "A Jewish pedlar hawking his goods in the streets of Vienna is more beautiful to me than an Austrian cadet."

"You don't know what you're talking about," Father had said.

"Yes, because you don't know the Austrians. I grew up in a military boarding school."

"And you, my friend, don't know the Jews. If you knew the Jews you wouldn't be so eager to join them. They're petit-bourgeois to the bottom of their souls. And their faith is petit-bourgeois too."

"And the Austrians? What do you think the souls of the Austrians are like? They make me sick."

And while the argument had been in full spate the bitter tidings came. Aunt Theresa, the most beautiful of all my aunts, had died in St. Peter's convent. Father made a very strange face and rose as if to close the open front window. Mother sank into her chair, and then started packing immediately.

I woke from my reverie and saw: the café was empty, the people sitting there had left. Stark's face was pale from all the cognac he had drunk. Father's face was red, as though this were not the threshold of death but a prologue full of exultant despair.

The waitress approached me and asked, "Aren't you tired, sweetheart?"

"No."

"How lucky you are that your parents take you out with them to have a good time. Will you remember me one day?"

"Of course I will."

"My name's Elsa. You'll always find me here. Your parents are very nice people."

Strange, no one interrupted our conversation. Father looked at me with a gratified expression: I was already capable of holding a conversation of this kind without being overcome by embarrassment.

Mother rose to her feet and said, "It's four o'clock." I was amazed at the extent of her practicality at such a time.

A heavy fog had settled on the avenue and the adjacent fields. Stray lights groped in the darkness. Mother dragged us down the narrow road to the station. Now I recalled the long night journey when we took Aunt Theresa to the sanatorium. Only then it had been summer, a fine cloudless summer.

The kiosk was now empty and deserted. The two dirty, closed windows revealed the mess inside: glasses and bottles.

"Where's the train?" called Stark in a compelling voice. The cognac seemed to have charged his voice with power.

There was no reply. An awkward smile spread over Mother's face, as if she weren't my mother, but one of those bitter women burdened with children, whose bodies are so used to pain that any new pain only twists their mouths.

"Station master, where's the train?" Stark called again in a thunderous voice.

The station master stuck his head out of the observation post and said, "What on earth brings you here at this hour?"

"We were told that a freight train came past here at five o'clock. Is it going to load or unload?"

"It's meant for freight, not people."

Stark's strange confidence lifted our spirits and gave us courage. But for Mother's face, the whole thing would have been almost like a nocturnal adventure.

At five o'clock the train pulled in. Stark climbed up to the engineer and told him that our sister, Aunt Theresa, a dearly beloved younger sister, had died that night in St. Peter's convent. He spoke loudly, pronouncing each word separately, to overcome the noise of the engine. From below it sounded like a grim proclamation. The engineer, sooty and tired, paid no attention to him apart from saying, "As long as you take the responsibility."

"Get in!" commanded Stark.

And while we were climbing up the planks, the conductor approached and stopped us. Stark tried at first to explain quietly, almost in a whisper, that we were a family in mourning, a family that had just received a heavy blow: a young, beloved sister had died in St. Peter's convent. The bitter tidings had reached us only a few hours before.

The man seemed touched. But suddenly, as if with malice aforethought, one of the guards appeared, half asleep, and announced that he was not going to let the wool be pulled over his eyes any more. He knew them well: they were Jews. He ignored our presence and addressed himself to the conductor. And the latter, who at first seemed embarrassed, considered for a moment, and said that he couldn't allow it. Stark, who all this time was alert but very controlled, went right up to the two men and drew himself to full height. They stood their ground.

"Get in," commanded Stark. The guard, who had apparently not expected any opposition, screamed at the station master, "The Jews are getting on without permission!"

"Don't say Jews, say people," whispered Stark. This remark was apparently too much for the guard. He took off his coat and said, "I'm ready to fight for my honor." Stark took his right hand out of his coat pocket and, sweeping it almost elegantly through the air, hit the guard in the face. Then he said quietly, in a smoldering voice, "That's an Austrian punch, pure Austrian. Acquired in the General Lunz Military Academy for Cadets, to be precise."

The results were obvious to all eyes: the guard lay flat on the platform, the conductor retreated from the train door, and the station master called out to them from the observation post, "What did you have to start up with innocent people for?"

"I'm not mistaken. They're Jews. I swear by all that's

holy," shouted the guard. The engine was already belching billows of steam. We climbed onto the train with the feeling that justice, when accompanied by a certain amount of strength, will eventually triumph over stupidity.

The purpose of our trip seemed to have been forgotten. Stark recounted various episodes about the illustrious military academy for cadets named in honor of the late General Lunz where small, weak creatures were forged into muscular bodies with no wills of their own. He had spent four whole years there. But for a few sensitive nerves and a few revolting sights, he would probably be serving today in the glorious 52nd regiment and rising through the ranks.

The enigma of the sculptor Stark grew even greater in my eyes. The freight train chugged slowly along. The cold wind from the fields penetrated our coats. Mother for some reason found it necessary to apologize, and said that while there had been several conversions in her family, and some well-known cases among them, in the last analysis they had not done it for reasons of faith, but because of circumstances.

I knew: these facts were not exact. I kept quiet and Father too did not correct her. I felt: she is forgetting herself because of the pain. The heavy predawn shadows pressed about us. And we sank into the moist down of the darkness.

After about an hour we were standing in the ancient baroque station of St. Peter's. A number of porters were dragging sacks from the freight cars, and a horseless cart, its shafts bowed, stood abandoned in the station entrance. A few veins of pink appeared on the horizon.

The gates of St. Peter's, wrought iron covered with brown veins, were locked. The darkness of the night was still clinging to the walls of the ancient buildings. The air was full of a broad, predawn calm.

Day broke and the single peal of a bell shattered the calm. The dreary wait next to the locked gates did not arouse any feeling of grief in us. The weariness of the night lay heavily inside us.

"They won't open before seven," said Mother, as if she knew all the secret ways of these walls.

"Why?" asked Stark.

"They only open after prayers. Strangers distract them from their meditations."

Mother appeared to know many secret details about the monastic life. She spoke about it warmly, as if she wanted to cling to Theresa's last thoughts. Father, who wanted to enliven the dreary wait, said, "You have to admit, they do show certain signs of true religiosity." This remark immediately aroused the weary Stark, who said, "Oh, undoubtedly—for anyone who doesn't know them."

At seven the gates opened. Mother asked to see Sister Victoria, and the gatekeeper went to call her.

The high walls of the antechamber with their pictures and statues enveloped us for a moment in their shadowy gloom. Even in times of catastrophe, we knew, entry into the convent was forbidden without a nun as escort.

Sister Victoria appeared with a flock of nuns, who surrounded Mother in a quiet not lacking in ceremony. This, apparently, was the way in which they received mourners. Mother did not ask where to go or what to do, as though the ceremony were at its height.

Immediately we found ourselves crossing the convent courtyard, gliding down corridors alternately dark and illuminated. It was not death we felt here but a hypnotic quiet that drew our feet forward. We reached the mourners' room, the narrow cell full of incense and flowers, without deviating from our course. Next to the coffin were two old nuns. They did not move aside.

Theresa's face in the coffin was made up with bright pink rouge, her braid lay on her neck. Her youth was innocent and flawless. Her hands too were carefully manicured, lying crossed on her breast. Quiet rested on her closed eyelids. Mother approached the coffin, her head slightly bent, as if she was looking into a baby's cradle.

While we wondered what they were going to do, the

seated nuns broke into a stressed, rhythmic chant, rolling the words out in a monotonous lament. Mother did not weep, but her face twisted as if she had a sour taste in her mouth.

When the ceremony was over, Mother turned her back on the coffin with a hasty, almost indifferent movement, fixing her eyes on Sister Victoria as if it were she who was the chief mourner.

"She died peacefully," said Sister Victoria.

"Suddenly?"

"And with no sign of pain."

"Thank God," said Mother.

And thus, without any overt awkwardness or jarring notes, the ceremony in all its little parts came respectably to an end. And since everything had gone so smoothly there was a general sense of satisfaction, which we too shared. We returned to the gates. Mother asked Sister Victoria if there was anything we could do to help. Upon hearing this whispered question the nun looked relieved. "Everything has already been taken care of," she said.

"We must go," said Father, as if we had another pressing engagement somewhere else.

"I'm coming," said Mother.

"As you wish," said Sister Victoria carefully.

I remembered that Uncle Karl, who later had an important literary prize named after him, had surprised the family by leaving his body to science. For some reason, however, they did not respect his last wish and had the body cremated; the next day a modest ceremony with music and poetry was held next to the urn.

We left without asking when and where the funeral would take place. Father and Stark held Mother's arms. She did not appear to need this support.

The journey home was equally strange. At the station Stark drank several glasses of cognac one after the other. He began talking loudly and incoherently, using a country dialect and coarse expressions from his military boarding school days. Father, at first glad of this distraction, began to fear a scandal. Mother too tried to persuade him not to make a spectacle of himself in public. The express saved us by arriving on time.

All the way home Stark cursed the Austrian army. His face was pale but resolute and full of a strange power. Father prevented a number of fights from breaking out by saying that a drunk man was not responsible for his actions and there was no point in arguing with him. Stark was drunk but refused to admit it.

When we arrived home Mother hurried to set the table. Stark had sobered up, but Father nevertheless said that he should be given strong coffee to drink. Mother went to make the coffee as if it were an important mission, one which she performed with mechanical movements and an expression of ritual solemnity on her face. For lunch she served sausages and eggs.

Stark stopped cursing the Austrian army. He told jokes about his father, who had been a junior officer for years; when he retired he used to talk to himself, barking out commands as if his platoon were standing in front of him.

After lunch he set out for Rabbi Weiler's. Father, who saw his efforts to return to Judaism as a piece of pure folly, refrained from needling him this time.

In the evening too Mother's movements remained frozen. Father sat in the salon and leafed through a book. The house was completely silent. In the end Mother asked whether she should make supper. These words were all she said, and besides them there was nothing else.

After supper Mother took off her shoes and sat on the floor. Her rigid face seemed to come alive. Father tried to stop her, but Mother said that she was perfectly comfortable on the floor.

I had a term test in algebra weighing on my mind. It was a difficult test, and I didn't know how I was going to pass it. Father tried his best to help me solve the equations. In the end he tore up the pages and cursed this abstract occupation, which did no one any good. Mother, sitting on the floor, watched us searchingly.

In time Father fell asleep in his chair. Mother closed her eyes and rested her head against the wall. They slept lightly, as if they had collapsed on the ground by a shady pool. I took two blankets and covered them. They slept as if they were floating, each in his own sleep, and I felt as if I had been cast up on a deserted shore.

The next day all the corners of the house were full of Theresa's death. Mother did not rise from the floor and Father brought her a cup of coffee, kneeling down beside her. I noticed: a yellow stain had appeared on her brow during the night.

When I came home from school the sculptor Stark was already sitting in his armchair, full of vitality and a little drunk. He spoke gaily and eloquently about Rabbi Weiler, the dear man who was studying Bible and Midrash with him. Father was not swept away by his enthusiasm, but merely remarked in an offhand kind of way that this opiate would not make his dry bones live. Stark did not seem to hear, for he went on talking with growing enthusiasm.

Our mourning was not over. The little arguments between Father and the sculptor Stark grew sharper. One evening when I was poring over my Latin books and Mother was standing by the wardrobe shaking naphthalene from the clothes, I heard Father raising his voice. "No one will be able to revive those Jewish ghosts. They're doomed to extinction." Now Theresa's death was felt in everything, even in the household utensils. All Mother's movements were very careful and seemed directed toward some goal clear only to her. Her movements made me anxious.

One evening Stark appeared, tall and thin, and announced that the rabbinical court in the nearby town of Schmieden had met in a special session to examine his intentions and his knowledge and had concluded that he was now entitled to go to the hospital in Vienna and be circumcised. As proof, he produced a little slip of paper with a square stamp on it, which he fished out of his waistcoat pocket.

Father was not pleased. Our reserved mourning seemed to withdraw even further into itself. In vain Stark tried to inspire us with his former confidence. The chill of mourning wrapped us in its silence. Mother's eyes were full, as if the grief had congealed in them.

The silence among us lasted a long time. In the end Father's sorrow burst out and he spoke of his incurable literary defects. The French again. Only the dispassionate French artists, Stendhal and Flaubert, only they were true artists. All we were good for was light verses and feuilletons. Father seemed to sense that his bitterness was about to drown him in words, and he clutched the cognac bottle like a staff in his hour of distress; in the bitterness of his heart he cried out in a fit of agony and compassion, "Why take this trouble on yourself, Kurt? You're a free man. Even your posture speaks of freedom. Your artistic heritage is one of freedom. Your father, an Austrian by birth, left you land, health, hands fit to carve stone, and you want to exchange this health, this freedom, for an old, sick faith. Take pity on your freedom, take pity on your body, which never had to suffer a senseless mutilation. Banish these evil thoughts from your mind. Believe me. You are dearer to me than a brother."

Mother started up and rose to her feet as if to stanch the flow of blood in Father's words. But Father was too drunk to stop. "Take pity on your precious hands, your hands that know granite and marble. Why should the rabbis mutilate your beautiful body?"

Stark did not try to stop this flood of words. His upper lip trembled and an embarrassment seemed to stammer on his face. Father's expression was full of a strange power. Stark made no reply. His eyes were fixed on Father's drunken hands. His look was green, but had no bitterness in it, as if a different understanding already dwelt in him.

The next day at seven o'clock we were standing on the station platform to see him off. A heavy rain was falling and the entrance was crowded with soldiers, trucks and workhorses. Father clung to Stark's arm, grumbling all the time about the fact that we had not taken raincoats. And in this confused mumbling we parted from him.

We came home wet. Father looked strange standing in his bare feet, the upper part of his body bare, cursing the railway timetable. Mother too stood barefoot on the cold floor, her toes red. Suddenly Father struck his head and said: "Why did I let him go? It's a crime. I shudder to think of what they are about to do to him." There was no power in these words, only a naked pain.

10

STARK'S departure still did not give us peace. Father paced the rooms like a caged animal, muttering, "Why did I let him go?" Our withdrawn mourning was tinctured with anger. And from twilight to twilight Father wrote letters, memos, express letters, and registered letters to his old publishers, who had stopped sending him money. Since none of them troubled to reply, he would spend most of the day standing by the window scheming, grinding his teeth and clenching his fists with a threatening grimace on his face.

The wind dropped and we set out to visit Stark. The day after his departure Father had already wanted to go after him and stop him from realizing his intentions, and even considered appealing to the sculptor's family to intervene and prevent this madness. But everything was still shrouded in Theresa's death. Mother sat on the floor, not eating, and Father stood over her threatening, pleading, "Get up."

Immediately after Stark's departure the rain poured down. Mother did not weep. She withdrew into herself. They did not speak at all, and if they did it was about Stark and the barbaric customs that claimed pieces of men's bodies.

Now the wind had dropped and we set out to look for Stark. Father wore a sporty outfit and Mother wore her clumsy woollen shawl; it was in clothes like these that Father used to go off to sue his slanderers. The journey was soon over—by noon we were standing at the entrance of the building.

The exterior looked as if it had seen better days. Now a few old men wrapped in blankets sat in the doorway letting the cold sunlight soak into their bones. In reply to Father's question they confirmed that this was indeed the Paul Gottesman Almshouse. The stairs and the front entrance looked neglected and frost-bitten. We found Stark lying side by side with a lot of old men in a hallway. A suffocating smell of disin-fectant and medicine filled the gloomy space. Two practical nurses, gentiles, joked raucously. Father's face suddenly twisted with revulsion. Mother shrank by his side, as if she was standing in a place where religious rites took place. There were a few candles flickering on the shelves that actually looked like ritual candles.

Stark stretched his hands out to us in a glad greeting. It was only when we stood next to him that we saw how he had changed. His face was covered with gray stubble, he had a shabby skullcap on his head and a little prayer shawl on his chest. Only his eyes held the old familiar spark. Father was stunned. He said, "I don't understand," and turned his head away, looking into the gloom as if he hoped to meet the eyes of the guilty there.

The place was in semidarkness. A few old men lay on their beds and others played cards by the light of an oil lamp. They seemed to recoil as they met Father's accusing eye.

"Everything went smoothly," said Stark in an apol-ogetic tone. His shaven head and the shabby skullcap gave him the look of a political prisoner.

"So this is where you've landed." Father could barely control himself. Stark, apparently sensing Father's sup-pressed rage, spoke to him softly. "It's not as bad as it looks. There are some devoted people here." And Father, apparently realizing that what had been done could not be undone, said, "I imagine so."

Mother sat on the empty bed next to Stark's, her eyes fixed on the wax candles. Our arrival had apparently caused something of a stir. One of the gentile nurses called out to the other end of the corridor, "Stark's got visitors." This announcement was greeted with youthful laughter, shattering like glass into thin splinters of derision.

And in the middle of our confusion and embarrassment, an old man dressed in a striped business suit approached the bed and bowed to Father with old-fashioned politeness. "Pardon me if I make so bold as to disturb you, sir," he said, "but necessity, as they say, is no disgrace." Then he added, in a tone that was not lacking in a certain theatricality, "I am here, sir, against my will."

"How can that be?" said Father, astounded.

"My son brought me here on the pretext that there was a Jewish atmosphere in the place. Look around you, please, at the Jewish atmosphere, which certainly exists here in abundance: dirt, the corruption of businessmen. All that's missing, unfortunately, is medical care. The doctor comes once a week, if that. And the nurses, to put it delicately, are busy with their own affairs."

"Why don't you leave?"

"I have been deprived of my freedom. My son does not want to give me back my freedom. And ever since he deprived me of my freedom, I am not at liberty to leave."

"But why did he do it?"

"His reasons, sir, are a mystery to me. To punish me, if I might hazard a guess."

"Couldn't he find a more suitable place?"

"I imagine that better places than this exist, but my son in the depths of his hatred for his father decided that this was the place for me. No other place would satisfy him."

"How can I help you?"

"I don't know. I was a businessman. A prosperous businessman. Popular with my customers and my peers. I was content with my lot. I lost touch, to tell the truth, with Jews. They were never to my taste."

"Is your son an orthodox Jew?"

"What put that idea into your head? He's married to a gentile."

"I don't understand," said Father, spreading his hands.

"Neither do I. Apart from his desire to see his father spend the end of his days in a Jewish almshouse."

The man straightened his shoulders and without another word turned toward the door. But he immediately stopped in his tracks, turned on his heel, and added, "Forgive me for troubling you with my private affairs. Forgive me. Sorrow sometimes makes people forget themselves."

The faint light filtering through the high windows grew stronger and spotlighted the beds lined up in two crowded rows against the walls. Of Stark's strong and hairy face nothing was left but the whiteness of the skin, a few pink spots, and a pale blotch on his forehead. Father held the head of the bed in both his hands and his eyes slid along the stripes of light crossing the ward.

"The man's right," said a voice. "The treatment here is beneath contempt. We too were deceived. We were promised great things, and now we don't even get soup for lunch."

"Who's in charge here?" Father's voice thundered.

"The administrator," said a voice from the annex.

"And are there no doctors here?"

"Only sometimes, they don't come regularly."

"I want to see the person in charge," said Father, and made for the dark annex at the end of the ward.

The light grew dimmer again. The candles spread their dark circles on the walls. Mother, for some reason, asked Stark if there was anything he needed. "I have everything I need. I'm learning to walk on my new legs. I've already taken part in a minyan and been called up to read the Torah, and in the evening we have Bible lessons." Mother nodded her head piously.

There was no shadow of beauty in this place, or

any gesture that could be regarded as religiously inspired. Everything expressed a veiled mockery, suspicion, a kind of gloating malice. The men who had
been sitting crosslegged on the beds playing cards now
sat drinking coffee out of little cups, baiting each other
in a babble of unintelligible words that sounded like
curses.

And while Mother tried to string together a few
words, the sound of Father's thunderous voice was
heard. "Where is the person in charge?"

The thunderous voice hung unanswered in the air.
The front windows narrowed their light, a dense darkness slid from the ceiling, and the candles on the
shelves stretched their flames sideways. None of the
men sitting on the beds made a move; the game had
resumed.

"Where is the person in charge, I asked," Father's
voice thundered again.

"He's still looking for him," said an old man and
threw a card onto the blanket.

"If the person in charge doesn't put in an appearance immediately I'll complain to the Ministry of
Health. This is a public disgrace."

This threat fell on deaf ears. In the illuminated doorway Father looked slightly ridiculous in his tight sports-
clothes. He turned toward the cardplayers sitting on the
bed. They looked at him and said, "Didn't you find
him?"

"No."

"He'll come. What's the hurry?"

"Isn't there an office here?"

"I think there is one. But what do you need an office
for?"

"I want to see the person in charge."

"Don't worry. He'll come. Be patient."

"What is this place, anyway?" Father stood still for
a moment.

"The gentleman wants to know what this place is."
Father's interlocutor turned to his friend.

"A Jewish almshouse, an almshouse. A venerable

institution. Haven't you ever heard of it here in Austria?"

"And what do you do here?"

"Explain to the gentleman what we do here."

His friend, who was absorbed in the card game, said without looking up, "What do we do here? We play poker, that's what we do here. It doesn't do anyone any harm, not even us."

And while the words flowed back and forth, words spoken in a tone of affected detachment and spiteful boredom, a tall man dressed in black, elderly and with a look of dignified poverty, appeared in the doorway.

"Here he is, you want to talk to him, don't you?" said the man on the bed, again without raising his eyes from the cards, as if Father were making a nuisance of himself.

Without waiting, in a rush that suggested uncertainty rather than authority, Father turned toward the door. "Are you the orderly in charge of this place?"

"Whom are you looking for?" asked the tall man, who seemed blinded by the darkness.

"I'm looking for the person in charge."

"I am he," said the man.

"I'm giving you notice: this is a public disgrace. This place is a stable and not a public institution. I intend to complain to the Ministry of Health."

"Why upset yourself?" said the man quietly.

"It's your responsibility."

The man opened his eyes and scanned the dormitory with a broad, calm, unresentful gaze, silencing all the little activities among the occupants of the beds.

"What do you want of the rabbi? He doesn't owe you anything," said one of the cardplayers, as if he were addressing a bully.

"I demand an explanation."

"Who are you anyway? Why don't you introduce yourself?" said one of the cardplayers in a provocative tone.

"I am an Austrian citizen. Isn't that enough?"

The elderly rabbi's broad gaze now took in all those

standing around the doorway. At last he looked at Father, as if to say, "Why are you distressing us so cruelly?"

"What have you done to this man?" demanded Father pointing defiantly at Stark, in a strangely theatrical voice, a nasty voice.

"Leave the rabbi alone, don't torture him," said a voice from within.

"I'm not interested in any of you. See what you've done to a great artist: a great artist in stone. An artist whose hands are worth their weight in gold."

"Leave the rabbi alone. He hasn't done anyone any harm."

"I won't leave him alone."

The last words set the match to the fire. From the darkest part of the dormitory a knot of skinny men came rushing out like a swarm of angry wasps and, hurling their weak bodies against Father, began pushing him out of the door.

Father clung to the wall, his arms outspread. They surrounded him like a black wall, shouting weakly, "Get out!"

"Please, we're all Jews here." The rabbi tried to deter them. He seemed to have a certain power over them but not absolute control. They would not desist, and with one concerted push, they shoved Father out of the door.

"Gentlemen," protested Mother, "is it right to hit people in a religious place?"

Father, beside himself with fury, shouted, "I don't want anything. All I want is the sculptor Stark, bewitched by your spells. He's the only one I care about. The rest of you can go to hell."

"Shut up."

"You ought to be ashamed of yourself."

"Assimilated Jew."

Stark rose from his bed and bounded athletically to Father's side. He took his arm and said, "This man is a well-known writer. One of the best known."

"Why did he insult the rabbi? Let him insult us.

There are plenty of good reasons for insulting us, but not the rabbi."

"He didn't mean it." Stark tried to protect Father.

"In that case let him apologize. Let him beg the rabbi's pardon. We don't need apologies. Nothing will help us any more. But the rabbi's something else."

"I don't need apologies." The rabbi dismissed them with a wave of his hand.

"But we won't let him get away with it." There was a bony strength in the black mob swooping vengefully on Father.

"I refuse to apologize for something I'm not guilty of," said Father stubbornly.

"You insulted the rabbi," insisted one skinny old man in striped pyjamas.

"That insult will pursue you for the rest of your life."

"No wonder people hate them," hissed Father.

"Apologize to the rabbi."

"I don't need apologies. Leave the man alone," said the rabbi and turned away. Suddenly the hostile knot seemed to come undone. The people went back to their gloomy beds and the rabbi spread his hands out in the smoky air as if he were trying to touch some invisible body. "What's the good of talking. It's a waste of words," said the old man in the striped pyjamas. Dense smoke rose from the wax candles on the shelf. Father looked down at the floor, ashamed and humiliated. Stark tried to rally him, but Father was absorbed in his own bitterness and did not utter another word. And even when we took our leave he did not say good-bye. Stark accompanied us to the front door. The skullcap and little prayer shawl now gave him the look of a tall businessman bowed under a weight of work.

"Alms, lady," said someone to Mother. She offered him a banknote and he kissed her hand and blessed her. Father's hands, previously so full of energy, hung limply by his sides. The beggar pounded on me too and asked:

"You know the Torah, little boy?"

"No."

"A pity," said the beggar. I did not know if he was really sorry, or if he was mocking. His face was expressionless.

For hours we wandered aimlessly through the dark alleys of the city. We drank coffee and ate sandwiches. In the end we sat in a little inn full of people and Father drank beer. Father said, "Beer refreshes me." I was surprised to hear him talking like this about himself.

Dusk descended early on the fences of the houses and lights went on in the windows. A long shadow, the shadow of the church spire, fell on the cobbled street and was swallowed up in the dusk.

"Did you see?" said Father suddenly.

"What?"

"What they're like. No wonder people hate them."

And we went on wandering in the empty streets, trudging through the gathering darkness. Father's unshaven face reminded me of a day laborer being led home drunk after the day's work.

And later too, in the train, he did not stop cursing the Jews infesting Austria like rats, infesting the whole world, to tell the truth. Mother tried to hush him. Her gentleness only increased his rage. Nor did Stark escape his wrath—anyone who went willingly into that den of animals was no better than they were.

For many days Father was sunk in gloom. His face was covered with yellow spots and a tremor shook his lips. Mother sought refuge among the hospital patients and poor souls locked up in asylums.

And when Father emerged from his gloom he shut himself up in his room and wrote, and in the evenings he read Theresa's letters. The lucid descriptions brought her back to life. Father thought they should be copied and brought out in a book, as a testimony to true religious feeling.

11

AUTUMN came and Father decided to put an end to the growing hostility surrounding us. We were already isolated, friendless, and bankrupt, deep in the heart of a cold, gray season. I was still going to school, doing my homework, and taking examinations; but everything around us was in a state of gay, drugged despair and the bitter smell of the approaching end was already in the air. My lessons, notebooks, and text books were like little madnesses in the midst of the increasing isolation surrounding us. Next door to our house boys and girls held riotous parties until late at night. In the early hours of the morning they would bang on our front door and shout, "Jews!"

The little town, previously so calm, tranquil, and tolerant, now seethed with a violent gaiety, and we lived in it like animals on display, mocked and abused. Not one of our many friends came to Father's aid. The Jewish–Christian League—in which Father had been an active member for years, and in the end the editor of its journal—closed down its offices. The property was sold in a public auction, and Father stopped getting invitations from the city council. The post box, once full of surprises—letters, journals, books—was empty but for the electric and water bills and warning notices from creditors.

Strange—Father was not angry with the friends who had abandoned him, the many societies that had stopped inviting him to their meetings. He was angry with the

Jewish petite bourgeoisie. He spent his time writing pamphlets attacking the Jewish petite bourgeoisie, saying that they should be stamped out because they were selfish, narrow-minded, and lacking in true feeling. This was now his sole, burning means of expression. He wrote in a frenzy, although nobody was interested in his manuscripts any more.

Mother withdrew into her own activities. She undertook a number of small duties and carried them out scrupulously: weekly visits to the hospital, collecting clothes for the orphanage. This was now her secret. But these modest activities brought her no relief. It was as if she were feeding some demanding devil, who wrung out of her not only her few pennies, but also her hidden feelings. Father grumbled, "I can't understand the point of this righteousness. You want to do it—do it. What's the big secret? Why do you keep things hidden from me?" Mother would stand there small and humiliated, as if she had been caught stealing.

And then Father decided that our isolation was intolerable. We had to get away. In Tyrol, he had a boyhood friend called Dauber, a member of the Austrian nobility. As students they had done much together to change the face of Austrian literature, brought out a journal and held literary parties. When Dauber completed his degree, he had taken over his parents' large estate in the Tyrol. He had kept up his literary interests for a number of years, and then he had become more and more preoccupied with his economic concerns and started dabbling in politics.

There were no grounds whatsoever for Father's hasty decision. He had not seen Dauber for years. He wrote two long, detailed letters and received no reply. Nevertheless he clung to the idea of getting away and insisted on going to visit his friend in the Tyrol. At first Mother tried to dissuade him, but he was determined. So she started packing the green suitcase. I noticed that she held her hands close to her body and her movements were constrained; and when she turned her head

to ask if she should pack the leather boots, there was
a sharp sadness in her look. Father was obsessed with
private yearnings, and in the grip of his obsession he
dragged us with him.

The ticket counters at the railway station were be-
sieged by soldiers and civilians. Two women stood
laughing loudly. Father looked strange standing to one
side with a sour smile on his lips, as if he realized the
hopelessness of pushing his way in, but couldn't bring
himself to say, "Let's go home, there's no hurry." Who
knows, I thought to myself, perhaps this was precisely
the way in which Aunt Theresa had smiled to herself on
the threshold of her final insanity: a kind of weary
reflectiveness spilling over onto the lips. Ever since
her death we were all living her life, fragment after
fragment. Even this rash journey, it seemed, was nothing but a meeting with that insanity of hers.

Now Father too shoved his way into the pile of people next to the ticket booth. We saw from close up
how he struggled to the counter. Time and again he
came close, even very close, only to be pushed back
to the wall with his hand still outstretched, before diving
into the whirlpool again. At last, when he was at the
counter and buying the tickets, one of the people standing there called out, without looking straight at him,
"I wouldn't allow them in." Father bent down to pick
up his hat, which had fallen off in the crush, and
tripped—and when he stood up again the man looked
right at him and called again, "I mean you."

Only Mother had a seat. For the first time in my
life I travelled in a third-class compartment, full of
smoke and the smell of beer, surrounded by people in
greasy overalls. We stood packed close together, exposed to the acid looks of the drunks. Father's country
dialect didn't help, and neither did his jokes: everyone
now knew that we were Jews—and what was worse,
Jews who tried to pass themselves off as Austrians.
Mother sat on the bench, her eyes wide open, as if she
had no more control over them, absorbing the voices
without the strength to close her lids. The monotonous

chugging went on for hours. And the longer we sat there the more the interest in us seemed to grow. Father, who tried at first to deny our origins, admitted in the end that we were Jews, but not merchants.

"And what about the Jewish merchants; shouldn't they be exterminated?" Someone's voice hit Father like a fist.

"Take note, please, the man is speaking of extermination," Father appealed to the other passengers.

"What do you suggest then? How do you think we should speak about the Jewish merchants?"

"I," said Father irrelevantly, "am an Austrian writer. German is my mother tongue. I have no other language. In German I have composed six novels, six collections of short stories, two books of essays. Haven't I brought honor to Austria?"

For a moment there was silence.

"Very nice. So why don't you go to the Jews and write for them? They must need writers. We'll manage with what we've got."

"Am I not an Austrian like you are? Didn't I go to school here? Graduate from an Austrian gymnasium, an Austrian university? Weren't all my books published here?" Father's bitterness flowed.

Here someone else intervened, a man with an ascetic face. "Just as I said. It's not only the economic life of the country they've taken control of."

"And what harm has the spiritual life done you?"

"If it's a Jewish spirit, it corrupts."

From the next compartment a voice said, "Enough talking. What's there to talk about?" The man with the ascetic face grimaced sourly, flushed, and said, "I'm not talking. He's the one who's talking." Mother's open eyes seemed to open even wider. She sat frozen in her seat.

The words stopped. They drank beer and sang songs—army songs and rude songs and songs cursing the Jews and their money. A tremendous power throbbed in their voices. Father drooped; even his right hand holding the strap looked humiliated. We heard our sentence in the songs. Father's face was trembling, but not with fear: only with pain. As soon as the train stopped he said, "Come, we're getting off here."

It was dusk. Mother stood in her old winter coat, a coat I was fond of, looking as if she had no will of her own left. Father dragged us into the little railway café as though there were a hailstorm raging outside.

The little café enveloped us for a moment in a warm, homey steam. Father spoke in his country dialect and the café owner responded politely and hastened to offer us hot coffee and rolls and butter. Father shook himself and said, "We've come a long way."

The year before, Father had received a letter, a warm letter, from a distant relative in South America. The letter was written in German, broken, but perfectly comprehensible. The relation invited us to come and join him there. The economic situation was not too bright, he wrote, but a man with initiative would not go hungry. The main thing was that there was no overt hatred of Jews there. The letter upset Father very much. To write to a famous Austrian writer suggesting that he go to South America and open a grocery store or a liquor business—wasn't that the height of Jewish impertinence? Only property. Only money. No respect for literature or music. The survival instinct above all.

How things had changed since then. But Father's determination to remain in Austria was even stronger than before. To leave at a time like this, with evil spirits raging, meant admitting that reason had lost out, that literature was to no avail. Father refused to leave, and his refusal had a hostile power: Let the entrepreneurs go. Let the petite bourgeoisie go. I could never stand them anyway. But we will not leave our posts.

Everything worsened, but Father clung to straws: omens and illusions. If a letter came from some remote reader praising one of his books he would read it over and over again and find good omens in it, and if he received a letter from a boyhood friend, converted or half-Jewish, who agreed with his opinions—he was as happy as if he had brought off a piece of fine writing. But hardly any letters came any more. And since there was no more money for court cases, Father would go out from time to time to try to borrow money from old friends—but they received him coldly. And then he thought of his friend in the Tyrol.

In the meantime the café owner brought rolls, butter, and cups of hot coffee. There was a simple domesticity about the place that reminded me of other times. Father recovered his voice and with it his plans: a liberal publishing house, a journal to fight the evil spirits. Only Dauber would understand—he was a fighter, an aristocrat, and a liberal at heart. He seemed to believe that the minute we reached Dauber everything would change.

But in the meantime we had to make our way from here to a station on the main line. The café owner knew nothing about railway routes and timetables. His calm peasant's face expressed the dull bewilderment of a man who had never wandered far.

Evening fell and the little station was deserted. The warehouses were shut and the side tracks were amputated at the closed warehouse doors. Father tried to encourage us with old, familiar words, but they had no power to lift the covering of futility from this empty silence. The thought that we would soon be swaying to the rhythm of a hostile country train brought no joy.

And just when all hope seemed lost, a little train came chugging out of nowhere and stopped at the station. It was late and the passengers were sprawled over the seats, reeking of beer. Father didn't bother to ask where the train was going. He was glad the people were sleeping. But he was wrong. One of them was awake and he soon spied us out, announcing at the top of his voice, "What are Jews doing on this line?" The other sleeping passengers did not wake.

Now I knew, for the first time, the look of the hunter. Something about us, a different complexion, exposed us immediately to these hunters. Unfortunately for us, the only free seats were next to the hunter who had spotted us at a glance.

"How can you be so certain?" Father attempted an objective tone.

"I know them well," said the passenger quietly, as if talking about some remote subject that had nothing to do with us.

"How?" inquired Father.

"From long observation. One observes and learns. Isn't that the way people learn?"

"And what are their distinguishing characteristics?"

"Oh, a great many. First, let's look at the obvious ones. They're shorter, aren't they?"

"And there aren't any short Austrians?"

"Yes. Of course. But it's not the same sort of shortness. Round shoulders. From never lifting heavy weights, you know. A shoulder like yours, for example, is very Jewish. Classically Jewish, one might say."

"Really? I never noticed," said Father, imitating the man's precise, matter-of-fact tone. "And is that all?"

"No. If you take only one feature into account you're likely to make a mistake. Even a serious, embarrassing mistake. You have to observe the look in their eye. The look in their eye tells you a lot."

"Interesting," said Father.

"The look in their eye is always anxious."

"What are they anxious about?"

"There's no creature on God's earth more anxious about his children than the Jew."

"A born Austrian isn't anxious?"

"A born Austrian isn't anxious by nature. He is a peasant by origin and gets his serenity from the marrow of the earth. His children grow up of their own accord. He never blames himself or anyone else."

"And these signs are enough?"

"No. Certainly not. But they're enough for the initial identification. Even though it's a long way from being complete yet. They've got certain facial expressions too—I'd call them basic, inherited expressions. I've discovered them, to my surprise, in cases of mixed descent too."

"You seem to be exceptionally discerning."

"All by dint of observation, my friend. A man looks and learns, no?"

There was no malice in his voice, only a kind of matter-of-fact detachment that did not appear to hold any fears for Father. Father interrogated him as if he were asking about a place or a mechanism, and the man answered him, trying his best to be accurate.

The people in the compartment slept, huddled in their coats. In the restaurant car, a few men sat with tankards of beer, withdrawn into themselves.

"What do you do for a living?" asked the man.

"Guess," said Father.

"A doctor, or a lawyer?"

"Almost right. I'm a writer."

"You write for the papers, I suppose."

"Journals."

"An intellectual, in other words."

After about two hours we arrived at a junction. No one else but us got off. Father parted from the man with a peculiar kind of gratefulness. Cold, winter lights drenched the deserted platform. Strange, I thought, the way we were passing through all these alien places. Like a scouting party sent ahead to reconnoiter unknown territory.

"A cup of coffee—I'd give my fortune for a cup of coffee." Father emerged from the labyrinth of himself and addressed us with polite affability. The kiosk was closed; the station master explained in a calm voice that at this hour everything was closed. Mother did not open her mouth. It seemed that she belonged to nothing but her own standing body: neither calm nor angry, but trailing after Father's nocturnal wanderings, Father who now wanted nothing but a cup of coffee. For a moment I was gripped by dread: Was it going to be like this always from now on, from one train to the next?

The train arrived. The coaches were empty, the first-class coach was empty too. And suddenly it seemed that we were back in the old days: comfortable, upholstered seats, green curtains, coffee served to the passengers in their seats. Like a nightmare bringing warm relief in its wake. Even Mother woke from her frozen state and said, "God, where are we?" Father joked, "Things aren't as bad as they seem. There are still trains fit for a human being."

But this relief lasted only about an hour. Once more we stood in a little station, a station with a single hut open to the wind and without any lights. Except for a weather-beaten old signpost with several names on it, including Dauber's, we would have been quite at sea. Father greeted the signpost joyfully. "Let's take our bearings," he said. "We must accustom ourselves to this new darkness."

We were already in the last watch of the night. Darkness oozed from the hills like a viscous fluid. Gusts of fog struck our cheeks. There was no sign of human habitation here, only the moisture of cultivated fields and the smell of manure. We trudged through the mud for a long time. Father carried the suitcase on his shoulders and walked ahead with long strides. And when the darkness grew dense and no direction emerged we paused next to a tree.

The estate, it transpired, was not far off. The morning light revealed it to us. "Yes, yes, when a man loses his faith his eyes are blinded," said Father to himself.

On a high hill, encircled by low hills, stood the house, or rather the group of houses. The morning light wrapped them in a fine mist of delicate shades of pink. The pastoral scene after our night of wandering held us spellbound for a moment. "We've come to the right place," cried Father, recovering his spirits. We were like people on holiday whose carriage had been delayed and who had decided to complete their journey on foot.

At the gates Father introduced himself as an old friend of the Prince's, a friend of his youth, a friend who had shared his youthful dreams and ideas. The gatekeeper, impressed by Father's country dialect, said in embarrassment that at so early an hour the Prince was still asleep. Father said, "If he hears that I'm here, he'll surely agree to get up. For years we were students together."

The gatekeeper hesitated at first, and in the end agreed to put through a call. The secretary said she had strict orders that she could not on any account disobey. She would agree only to take down the details and bring them to the Prince's notice at the first opportunity. Father laughed. "He's sleeping!"

The gatekeeper's lodge, a wooden cabin, had warmed up in the meantime. He gave us coffee and country bread, and Father told him again about the good old days in Vienna when he and the Prince had been students together. The gatekeeper, marvelling at every word, asked for more details, and Father did not spare them. Mother took off my wet shoes and dried them by the stove.

Two hours passed, and the telephone did not ring. Father wanted to put through a call to the house. Perhaps the secretary had forgotten. The gatekeeper hesitated, but in the end he agreed.

There were other priorities, the secretary replied. She had noted our request, and when she had an answer she would contact us. This answer still held out some kind of hope, some kind of promise, and the gatekeeper was still polite. He offered us dried fruit. The autumn sun, cool but pleasant, carved a low path over the estate, and the wet smell suggested whitewashed rooms, a roaring fire, and hot, milky dishes.

Morning passed and the vapors hanging over the fields dispersed. Noon came and went and there was still no call from the house. Now it was necessary to bribe the gatekeeper with a bar of Swiss chocolate before he would agree to put through a call to the secretary. Her reply was unambiguous: she did not wish to be troubled any further in this matter. When she had an answer she would contact us. The gatekeeper apologized, asked her to forgive him, and promised that in future he would follow instructions.

The gatekeeper's face changed color. Father gathered the shreds of his self-respect and said, "I'm not waiting here forever. Friendship is not a one-way street. A man is not a dog. Forgive us, sir, for troubling you." He addressed the gatekeeper with exaggerated respect, but the latter, apparently afraid of getting involved, did not reply.

Mother said nothing. We returned to the station, trailing behind Father's quick pace. Except for us there was no one to be seen in the cultivated expanse. Although everything that happened had a burning reality, to me it all seemed like a bad dream, as if we were walking through the green, windy landscape of a nightmare, struggling to put one foot in front of the other because of the heavy coils of sleep encumbering us.

When we reached the station the last light was already glowing on the tiled roof. Father's coat was spotted with mud and his face was frantic. "We're getting out of here on the first train," he said, as if we had any other choice.

Father's humiliated pride seemed strange in the deserted little station. There wasn't even a guard. Fast, grand trains sped past one after the other without stopping. A freight train too passed without stopping. And when evening fell and the guard came, Father fell on him as if he weren't a lowly guard but the person in charge of the railway schedule. The thin man smiled, apologized, and said that he was only the guard. There was a train at nine o'clock that would take us all the way home, if we had the patience to wait. Father was appeased and recovered his composure.

"Where from?" asked the guard in the country dialect.

"A visit to the Dauber estate."

Because the guard was civil and did not hold the angry outburst against him, Father offered him a bar of chocolate; the guard reciprocated by offering the information that no one had used the little station for days. It was far from the village, and the Dauber estate had its own transport. Mother asked for a drink of water and the guard produced an old jug and offered it to her. He thanked Father for the chocolate and bemoaned the new regulations, the worthlessness of the currency, and the declining morality of the young girls. It was all because of the evil winds blowing from the city. Father listened attentively; when he asked for a cup of coffee the guard apologized and said that he had once had a table and facilities for making coffee here and everyone was invited to drink his fill. It was obvious that the man was lying, but Father did not care: he was glad of this boastful nonsense—it was a sign that, in the eyes of the guard at least, he was still the master.

At nine o'clock the train arrived. The guard lifted the case into the compartment. Father parted from him as from a faithful old servant.

The train rushed into the dark. In the corners tired people slumped, huddled into their coats. A dull light poured from the rounded ceiling. Sadness descended on Father and his face was enmeshed in a new network of shadows. Suddenly I knew: he would not come out of this night whole.

The woman sitting next to us asked, "Are we far from Knospen?" Father extricated his head from its net of sadness as if a tender hand had wakened him. "Not far, Madame, not far."

She was a young woman. Her face in the dim light looked pretty. She asked Father if he were familiar with the route and Father, aroused from his sadness, spoke in detail and with a kind of affectionate eloquence about the scattered villages—where you could find the best wine, the finest roast beef, the most authentic atmosphere.

The woman laughed coquettishly, as if he were not relaying well-known facts but whispering charming secrets in her ear. And when he revealed to her that he was the writer "P.A." her mouth fell open, she clutched his hand and said, "I don't believe it." It appeared that she had read all Father's books, as well as the criticism, including Stefan Zweig's well-known essay.

"And now nobody's got a good word to say for me," said Father lightly.

"They'll live to regret it," she said.

Released, Father broke out of his meshes, laughed, and told anecdotes. He spoke about Stefan Zweig, Wassermann, and Schnitzler, the Vienna group and the Prague group, and about the writer who had great things in store for him—Franz Kafka. Father was drunk with words. It seemed that the sole purpose of our journey had been to meet this woman, so that she would provide him with a little feminine admiration. Mother and I seemed to have been forgotten. The more the coach swayed the more I sensed his attraction to the woman was growing. He spoke to her like a young man, as if nothing else existed.

About the Dauber estate he said nothing. He told her that he was in a hurry to finish the last chapters of his new novel. He tried to give his voice the non-chalance of a successful man. "Sometimes a writer needs an anonymous meeting," he said, "an anonymous audience, and sometimes fascinating encounters take place in the night."

Mother's frozen face grew attentive. She watched Father coolly, as if he wasn't her husband but a strange man trying to ingratiate himself with a woman.

The rest of the journey passed in silence. Father fell hand, twitching in time to the jolting train, expressed a strange happiness, as if he were drunk. Only his left hand, twitching in time to the jolting train, expressed dejection, as if it did not belong to his relaxed body.

We walked home from the station. Father's face was flushed and eager, he walked with long strides—the way he used to walk on his way to meetings of the editorial board. I sensed: Mother and I were like heavy, swollen limbs attached to his body. Without us he would be lighter.

And when we came home the atmosphere was embarrassed. Father hurried to remove his shoes, and while doing so he made the following remark: "Dauber will regret it. I'll never forgive him. I still have my admirers." His humiliation was now overlaid with a brisk and foolish expediency.

And in the morning the new estrangement we had brought back with us from the roads was already blowing through the rooms: a white, austere, silent estrangement. No one seemed to wonder where it came from. The line above Mother's upper lip now moved jerkily, like a gash trying to join itself together again. And although we had spent the whole night travelling Mother said severely, "Why don't you go to school? You have a Latin test." I knew that she did not want me at home at this difficult time. And when I was standing at the threshold with my satchel on my back I perceived that over her wounds a new pride had begun to spread.

12

IN the last days at home, which we did not know were the last, our door stood open and strange people walked in and out as if the house were a public hall. Mother stood in the kitchen making sandwiches. These people were panicked Jewish businessmen seeking a momentary refuge in their flight. Hunted girls came too, older than their years, with bitter, powder-caked lines making their faces look like flowers browned at the edges; and women with little children too; and other lost faces with the grime and soot of trains already clinging to them; and respectable old men. In their eyes our house was an island not yet inundated by the waves of catastrophe. Strange, not one of them knew how to explain what had happened. How they had arrived in our town, at our house, and where they intended to go next. Some were still neatly dressed, while the clothes of others smelled dankly of sweat and grease. Here as in every place exuding the stench of disaster, here too people occupied themselves with barter: the exchange of rumors and bitter jokes.

Even now Father clung to his illusions. He wrote, polished his manuscript feverishly. All his rage was turned inward against himself, against the flawed creations of his spirit. He shut himself in his room and worked day and night, struggling against the evil spirits that had not stopped beating on our door since the summer.

While everything buzzed with disaster, two letters

came from Vienna and inspired Father with new hope. These letters, it appeared, came from the Baroness von Drück, a friend of Father's youth, who had revived her literary salon and had obtained a great sum for the publication of a literary journal.

Mother was not glad. She knew these were nothing but autumn mirages mocking Father's fantasies. She did her work dutifully: a daily visit to the hospital, a weekly visit to the orphanage, and sandwiches for the panic-stricken salesmen and shopkeepers who continued to arrive on our doorstep. Mother withdrew even further into her activities and would not give up a single one of them. There was no joy in these activities, only persistence in the execution of duties that seemed to have been imposed on her from without. Father was no longer with us. He was in the grip of a darkness that seemed about to overwhelm him.

There was an old age home in the town, very run down, which over the course of the years had been completely neglected. The old men would sometimes invade the streets and beg for alms. Cantankerous, proud old men, who struggled with the municipal inspectors. One cold autumn day carts came and collected the old men. The carts moved in a procession down Hapsburg Avenue. The old men waved skinny arms, their waving hands expressing a malicious triumph. They had apparently been promised better conditions elsewhere, and they believed these promises. The convoy proceeded slowly to the railway station. Mother stood at the gate and watched them until they disappeared from view. No one knew what this uprooting meant, but Mother must have sensed something, for, after the old men were taken away, she devoted herself to distributing clothes and making sandwiches with a new zeal. A strange, self-denying piety infected all her movements, as if she were purposely imposing hardships on herself.

One evening she came home from the local orphanage with Helga, a girl my age. The orphanage was about to be transferred, and Mother decided to adopt the girl.

She was not particularly pretty or appealing. Her face was unformed and there was something dull about her brow. But apart from this there was nothing wrong with her. And thus she too joined the turmoil of the last days. No one imagined that they were actually the last days; only Mother's demonstrative charity made me suspicious. She would scold the wandering shopkeepers as if they were not strangers but her own flesh and blood who had to be kept in decent order. She gave everything she had to give, but she didn't give lightly.

And even in the final upheaval I went to school: plebeians and patricians. Equations with two variables, and those eternal kegs with two taps that never seemed to empty. Tests every week and fortnight so that nothing would get lost, even now. Mother watched over my homework with a vigilant eye.

And at night Helga would tell me about the extraordinary world of the orphanage, about the long bedrooms called dormitories, about the dining room that was also used for celebrations, the bitter matrons, and the laundry worker who could not keep his hands off the girls. She spoke simply, as if she were telling me facts of life. Sometimes a shrewd smile would spread over her face, like a young girl who already knew a secret or two worth knowing. But above all, she feared school; and if she had secretly hoped for liberation she now knew that, in this respect at least, nothing had changed. In the afternoons she would help Mother make sandwiches or distribute clothing. In her short life, transferred from one orphanage to another, she had learned to adjust to everything, and here too she tried above all to appear content.

One day Helga was caught stealing. Only a few pennies, not even enough for a box of chocolates. But Mother was very severe with her. I remember that she said to her, "We are not wealthy, but we do keep up certain standards. No one can take that away from us."

Helga cried, beat her fists on her head, swore that she would never again take anything that did not belong to her. That night she confessed to me that it was not she herself who had taken the money, but the devil inside her who sometimes took control: she was not a thief. She knew it was wrong to steal. The way she spoke about herself was very strange. One day she asked me if we were Jews.

"How did you guess?"

"I guessed. The Jews are spoiled, aren't they?"

"How do you know?"

"That's what they said in the orphanage."

"And what else did they say?"

She giggled and said, "I can't repeat it, it's not nice."

"And you, are you Jewish?"

"I don't know," she said, and giggled again. "We foundlings have no parents, we don't know who we belong to."

I soon learned that she had words of her own, words that made her laugh and words that brought a cunning expression to her lips. Mother did not spare herself and at night she would sit with Helga over her lessons. Helga's handwriting was heavy and deliberate, as if she were engraving the letters onto the paper.

And while the uproar was at its height—frightened shopkeepers, women who had lost their husbands, hunted girls, and Mother in the kitchen making sandwiches—Father called me to his room. He seemed very strange then; there was something alarming about the way he looked. He spoke about his writing and his unpardonable defects. He was excited and feverish and he tried to drag me too into his dark labyrinths. He spoke about Kafka and about the hidden nucleus that every artist seeks and that only Kafka had discovered. Ever since then all writing had been an insult. I knew: he was telling me about the oath he had sworn to the beliefs of his youth and to the pedantic devil who would not leave him alone. Suddenly he stopped talking. He had lost the words and me along with them.

One after the other the institutions in the town were liquidated: the insane asylum and the charity home for the paralyzed. The carts that had previously taken the old men away now took the insane and the paralyzed.

The convoys passed our house, and the quiet on their lost faces hung in the air for hours afterward. And at night the autumn cold seeped into the walls of the house.

Helga kept on asking me if the Jews had secrets, and if so what they were. She knew how to keep a secret, and would not tell anyone. There was cunning in her voice, like a girl who knows that life holds many secrets. She now wore a tight poplin dress that Mother had taken in to fit her properly. It suited her.

But she would not stop torturing me. "Tell me about the secrets, tell me. I won't tell anyone."

"There aren't any secrets."

"Why are you lying to me?"

"There aren't any secrets; if there are, I don't know them."

"But there must be something. Why don't you ask?"

I was amazed at the sharpness of her reactions and at the way she laughed. But for the Latin and arithmetic no one could have called her stupid. It was only books and exercises that terrified her. She would press me, "You must know something. Why won't you tell me? Aren't we friends?"

"Do you people believe in God?" The question was abrupt and surprising.

"No."

She sniggered and said, "Now I understand."

"What do you understand?"

"The truth."

"What's the truth?"

She laughed a secret, ugly laugh.

I knew that in this little town we were fair game for everybody. Even Mother's charity, her efforts on behalf of others, were held against her. Never mind Father, a man who sat shut up in his room all day long writing. Our sentence nonetheless was carried out with a certain discretion.

One day Helga came home from school with her face scratched, her satchel torn, and her hair tangled. She had been fighting with the girls for calling her a Jew.

"And what did you say to them?" asked Mother.

"I hit them."

"And what did they do?"

"They swore at me and hit me."

And thus our suffering infected her too. She fought for her life with the meager resources at her command. But nothing helped. The secret she had tried to pry out of me was already part of her. She may not have been aware of it, but she had changed in her months with us. She continued stealing, coming home late, fighting in the street. But now she hastened to confess, ask forgiveness, and weep for her little sins. Mother did not receive her confessions lightly, or forgive her lightly; and once she even said to her, "That is not the way to behave, Helga. That is not how we expect people to behave here."

Sometimes it seemed to me that one day she would run away or start spreading slanderous lies about us, especially since Mother was so strict about homework, memorizing, and all the other tasks she had previously performed so casually. But she did not run away. Her fate was sealed with us. Her movements grew more restrained, her fingers whitened, and a different, thin kind of smile now clung to her bony jaws. And in the evenings she would sit and listen, as if she were being initiated into a new world. Her questions stopped. Mother would tell her about other times, when everything was different and being a Jew was not considered a disgrace.

Helga did not say, "I am happy here. I want to stay with you." Nor did Mother say, "You will be better off with us." The decision, if there still was one, was up to her. Sometimes it seemed that she was about to leave us, to go anywhere where there was no school, to be a waitress in a restaurant or a cleaning woman at the railway station. But in the end she did not leave, perhaps because she had lost something in our house, that animal vitality that makes men brave.

Father would sometimes emerge from his room and shout, "Stop torturing the girl. People can live forever

THE AGE OF WONDERS • 123

without Latin or algebra." But these were only words. He was totally absorbed in his fantasies about the Baroness von Drück: the revival of Austrian literature, journals, books, a popular library to fight the evil spirits of the time.

And thus, without anything being decided, heavy days came upon us, days charged with moisture, the days before a storm. No one imagined that the storm was already on its way. The autumn light was in its full beauty, cold and clear, the businessmen came and went, and Mother did not forego a single visit to the charitable institutions that still remained open. She kept a strict timetable. There was no cash left in the house, but there were still plenty of clothes.

One evening an old friend arrived on our doorstep. Doctor Baum of the Jewish–Christian League, a tall man with deliberate movements. For weeks we had not seen a Christian friend in our house. Father greeted him warmly, he sat down in his usual place and without any preliminaries started reading aloud from a liberal petition: there were Jews and Jews, not all Jews were merchants. A list of Jewish intellectuals who had contributed to Austrian culture should be drawn up. All the parasitic elements should be dealt with ruthlessly.

Father sat and read the articles of the petition. The thought that there was still someone who had not abandoned him lifted his spirits for a while and he said, "The guilty will pay the penalty; I understand." I knew: we were under indictment, and the man with the deliberate movements was one of our judges. He sat for a while, and his dry northern look dripped into me with a cold terror.

That night we did not sleep. Helga woke up with a violent toothache and she wailed, threw herself about on the floor, and cried that she wanted to die. Mother went out and knocked on the clinic doors, but no one was prepared to receive us in the middle of the night. The next day the dentist pulled out her two front teeth. Helga lay on the couch in the salon, her mouth swathed in bandages.

How ignorant we were of the approaching end the following facts will testify: Father prepared himself to go to Vienna and help the Baroness von Drück revive her literary salon, Mother labored to set up a new home for the paralyzed and a soup kitchen for tramps. They quarrelled ceaselessly. There was nothing about which they were in agreement. The polite, delicate silence that had once reigned in our house was broken into bits. The smell of mothballs and moldy old books filled the rooms with an autumnal suffocation. No one cared any more about anyone else's feelings. Helga was miserable without her front teeth. She kept her nose in her books and studied until late at night. But her efforts bore no fruit. Now too her grades were humiliating. I did well at school, but nobody praised me for anything, as if it were taken for granted that I had to excel, or at least hold my own.

Since nobody knew that these were the last days in this house, on this street, and behind the grid of this lattice, which continued to cast its damp shade on the pavement, since nobody knew, everyone buried himself in his own affairs as if there were no end to this life. Father kept his literary delusions to which he continued to cling even when everything teetered on the edge of the abyss. He kept on writing and rewriting sentences and paragraphs, as if they were not words written on a page but crimes that could not be left unpunished. Mother too showed herself no mercy. From morning till night she worked, and in the evenings she would sit with Helga over her homework. Nobody cared now about anybody else's feelings. Only poor Helga, always an exception, was treated kindly by all.

13

"TAKE your raincoat"—these were the last words Mother said to my father. Even her bitter anger could not suppress them. But Father paid no attention and rushed out into the dark. No one went after him and his footsteps were swallowed up in the damp darkness with a soft, squelching sound. I sat in the salon doing my algebra homework, my adopted sister Helga sat by the piano. Everything had happened in a flash, as if lightning had struck through the window and blackened the familiar furniture.

The next morning Mother sat in the salon, her dressing gown zipped up to her chin, her face naked of makeup and a cup of coffee beside her. The green light of the gown made deep lines on her chin. My adopted sister Helga and I set out for school as if we had been rebuked. Religious instruction was taken from Father Mauber. We were reading St. Teresa of Avila's "The Way of Perfection." Suddenly I saw my father, a barefoot stranger, climbing up a mountain path, climbing and stumbling.

When I came home everything was as usual. A thick, autumn light lay in the pile of the carpets. Mother had taken off her green gown and was wearing a dress. I sat down to do my homework without saying a word. At five o'clock the Committee for the Advancement of Literature, of which Father was a member, met in the salon. Father's place next to the chairman stood empty. The subject under discussion was a manuscript that would have been worthy of encouragement but for a couple of pornographic chapters. There were some dry disagreements. The chairman took his stand on the first article of the charter, which said, "for the encouragement of beauty and good taste." It was decided to postpone the decision. The chairman and members of the committee signed the protocol. Mother served coffee and cheesecake.

No one mentioned Father's hasty departure. Everything proceeded as usual. Meals were served on time and Father's place at the head of the table was kept open for him. Mother stopped eating with us. On Saturday a registered letter arrived, addressed to me. I recognized Father's handwriting. He inquired about my health and Helga's health. He asked me to send him his mail and the books on the desk and to make a separate parcel of his manuscripts. He had enclosed a document giving me the power of attorney to accept his registered mail. The address on the back of the envelope was, Vienna, Masaryk 5. I sensed that Mother did not want to read the letter. That night Helga asked if I wouldn't like to join my father in Vienna. She seemed to have no sense of the confusion in which we were caught.

The cold grew more intense and in the back rooms we kept the blinds down. The house was in semidarkness all day long. No one asked why. We had a secret agreement not to talk about it. The dreadful rumors about divorce had not yet penetrated the house. Our little tragedy slid like damp wool around us.

Another letter arrived from Father, once more addressed to me. Again he did not mention Mother or ask how she was. Helga now brought spiteful stories back from school. The girls said he had a baroness in Vienna. And some claimed even worse: an opera singer of doubtful morals. Helga laughed and her laughter hurt me.

The date of my bar mitzvah approached and Mother asked me if I didn't think we should go and see the rabbi. I was surprised: she had never set foot in a synagogue before. Why now? I submitted without an argument. The next day we went to the rabbi's office. There was no beauty in the streets. The pretty, neat little town was overcast by damp clouds. There was an intermittent drizzle. We walked quickly through the streets. Mother spoke with restrained sorrow about Helga's poor grades. The piano teacher, too, was dissatisfied.

The rabbi asked for our family name with a certain reluctance, as if he did not trust us. Mother, who never spoke about her mother, now mentioned her name. The rabbi took out a card and asked many questions. In the end he raised his eyes, blue-black eyes, and surveyed us. It appeared that our words had not touched his heart. He said, "A home in which the religious precepts are not observed and the sons are not circumcised does not deserve to be called a Jewish home." Mother rose and drew herself up to the full height of her humiliated pride. She said, "We are Jews even without the rabbi's consent." The rabbi put the card away in a file and said, "In that case why did you come?" Mother flung her scarf over her shoulder and said, "To see for ourselves that our place is not with false priests."

The visit pained her. From then on until the day she died I did not see a soft line on her face. She kept busy and her devotion knew no bounds, a woman whose whole life consisted of giving. In December our own needs grew smaller and smaller. Mother stood by the sink cooking, washing dishes, and doing the laundry. Helga made no progress at school, and Mother sat for hours helping her with her homework. In December too a couple of committees still met in our house. The Committee for the Advancement of Literature, named after my uncle, did not approve the grant to the young writer. In the end the committees stopped meeting in our house. Mother's love was not gentle, but she was ours as she had never been before. Father's letters came every week, addressed to me. In one of his letters he wanted to know whether Mother would object to a visit from him. I did not dare ask her.

We celebrated my thirteenth birthday without much ceremony. We had no family in town. Our friends had withdrawn. Helga baked a cake and wore a party dress. Mother played some Mozart sonatas in honor of the occasion.

One after the other the publishers sent back Father's manuscripts. And in one of the accompanying letters they said quite clearly: Austria needs a different kind of literature, a healthy literature. From America too he received a refusal.

The end-of-term exams were easy. My report was resplendent with brilliant achievement. Mother did not even kiss my forehead. Her sole concern was now with Helga. Helga experienced great difficulty with Latin and arithmetic. Analyzing the syntax of a sentence made her sweat blood.

Occasionally an old friend, or a former maid, would turn up on our doorstep. Mother was now distributing clothes to charitable organizations. The lofty rooms emptied, of their own accord it seemed. I wrote a letter to Father and copied out my end-of-term report.

Helga brought back some new gossip: Father was living with the Baroness von Drück and had revived her literary salon. He had been seen in the company of the baroness wearing a hat with a feather. I knew: there was more than a grain of truth in these rumors, but nevertheless I was angry with Helga for such frivolous, irresponsible gossip.

Slowly but surely the evil days came closer. I was expelled from the gymnasium and no reason was given. Helga came home with a very bad report card, and a grave warning that if she failed the reexaminations she would be expelled at once.

Winter came before its time. Our living space was confined to the two front rooms. Helga walked around book in hand all day long. Mother made her recite formulas until late at night. Two reexaminations, in Latin and math, lay in wait for her like Angels of Death. Poor Helga beat her head with her fists. At the beginning of February we accompanied Helga to school. It was snowing heavily and we slipped through the streets like thieves. We waited outside, shivering. After about an hour Helga came out, as light as a bird. She had passed the tests, the certificate was in her hand.

That night Mother made Helga a pleated skirt. Helga chattered wildly. In the end she fell asleep, exhausted. I sat up with Mother until late at night.

The next day we received a registered letter from the rabbi's office: all members of the community were requested to present themselves in the courtyard of the temple at five o'clock on Tuesday.

"What have I to do with them?" asked Mother with a deliberate dryness.

For a whole day we ignored the letter. It had nothing to do with us. Then Mother ironed, and baked a cheesecake—as if she were getting ready for some occasion. On Tuesday we put on our best clothes and set out. We did not know how short the way was from our house to the temple.

The temple door was open and next to it in the courtyard stood a few people in winter clothes, umbrellas in their hands. They looked like merchants standing outside a wholesale shop. There was no dignity in the way they stood, only a kind of nervousness in their feet. We did not know a single one of them. Helga asked if there was going to be a ceremony, and Mother said with an abstracted air that she had no idea.

At five o'clock exactly, the rabbi appeared. He was wearing a dark coat and his square white beard gave him a proud, erect look. He went up to the temple door and beckoned the people to enter. They went in slowly and unwillingly. The light from the upper windows gave the hall a cold, ceremonial air. The rabbi approached the ark and stood opposite it for a moment in silence.

"What are we doing here?" someone asked in an astonished voice.

There was no reply to his question. The rabbi took off his coat, went up to the lectern, and pushed it aside with a mechanical gesture, as if his hands were used to making this movement. Then he sat down. A few women stood in the doorway peering into the darkness. They came in hesitantly, as if they were interrupting a ceremony. Helga shivered and Mother held her trembling hand. "Why are you shivering?" said Mother. "The exams are already behind you."

After about an hour the temple door was closed. A few lamps in the dome were lit. The rabbi rose from his place as if he had been waiting for a signal. He went up to the lectern next to the door of the ark and lit two candles.

He spoke in a moderate tone about the unity of the Jewish people, forged through adversity. The words rang sonorously from his mouth, as if we had not been brought here by official letters but had come of our own free will to worship our creator.

He spoke for a long time. And his voice, the voice of an old man, boomed powerfully in entreaty and reproach. Suddenly the front door burst open and an elegantly dressed woman was thrown inside. She opened her mouth as if trying to scream, but on seeing the rabbi standing on the rostrum the words froze on her gaping lips, she fell to the ground and crawled on all fours to the back benches. There was a stunned silence. Mother hurried over to help her. The woman stood up and drove Mother away with an angry wave of her hand.

The rabbi ignored the interruption and continued. Now the words thundered from his mouth. He spoke of bygone days, of the present decline, and of the repentance that would transform us utterly.

One after the other people were thrown inside. Some were hurt and others were wearing dressing gowns. Two children carried satchels. The rabbi descended from the rostrum and withdrew to his corner. The light pouring from the dome made us small. But no one went and banged on the door to get out. Their anger was directed against the people sitting in the

front rows—as if they were to blame for the catastrophe.

"Where's the rabbi? Where's that criminal?" shouted
someone.

Mother stood next to us, tall, proud, and with a kind
of cold composure. She had not yet given way to fear.

After the shout, an uproar broke out. Like animals in
a cage. Old words, once put to other uses, flew through
the air like falling soot. The anger of the people was
turned against the rabbi. The rabbi did not move. It
was as if he understood his sentence had now been
passed.

One after the other the lamps on the dome were ex-
tinguished and only the two candles on the lectern
threw their light in toward the darkness. Now the
hostile looks were open. Looks that already knew the
truth but were not yet resigned to it.

"I've never been in here in my life." A woman
wept bitterly. "Why am I here, why?"

"You're Jewish, that's why," someone hissed.

The door was locked with a bang and we were
prisoners in this temple in which we had never before
set foot. Helga cried and Mother did not try to comfort
her. And among the bitter words we heard were some
that were like nails driven into us and our private disaster. Someone knew that Father had abandoned us to
go and live with a baroness in Vienna. Someone even
mentioned the baroness by name. Someone else added
meaningfully, "Of course! It's all because of the degenerates. The decadent artists."

A woman hissed, "Don't forget, there's a bastard
girl amongst us too."

Mother brandished her umbrella and cried, "Shopkeepers!"

But these voices were only a distraction. The anger
against the rabbi increased. There was no longer any
doubt. Tonight judgement would be passed.

The rabbi did not beg for his life. He sat in his
corner wrapped in his prayer shawl, and this only made
the anger worse. The candles went out and a thick dark-

ness fell from the skylights. We huddled together on the floor, Mother, Helga, and I. We saw the merchants crawling toward the ark. The rabbi did not cry out. All night long they tortured him: hoarse voices tearing at the darkness like blunt saws.

And when light broke through the skylights the rabbi was lying on the floor, panting and bleeding. The torturers retreated to a corner and squatted on the floor. The rabbi did not cry out or accuse anyone. Snow fell on the skylights. The light dimmed. Mother took off her fur coat and covered us. The silence of an aftermath gathered the people together on the floor. Now no one said, "You, or you." Now no one probed our hidden wound. Their hostile looks blurred, as if the colors had melted in the irises of their eyes. The alien hall was filled with vapors from the people's mouths. Someone lit a cigarette and his hand shook like a prisoner's. A woman vomited. The rabbi's face was red, as though tattooed with fire. No one stretched out a hand to beg his pardon. The torturers squatted in their corner and stared dully at their victim.

By the next day we were on the cattle train hurtling south.

BOOK TWO

Many Years Later
When Everything Was Over

1

AT the end of April Bruno returned to the town of his birth. The train from Vienna to Stahlheim was full. A short Jew wearing a black skullcap sat next to him and spoke to him in German with a strange diction. All Bruno's attempts to ignore him only increased the stranger's flow of words. The man told him about himself, his business affairs, his wife, and his daughters.

The train raced north. The man ate, said a blessing, and made calculations on narrow strips of paper. In the end he went back to his mutterings, as if Bruno were a junior partner in his business, and perhaps also in his troubles. The other passengers stared at his alien gestures, but their stares apparently did not bother him. He spoke aloud, as if he were chewing the words. Bruno could not stop himself from saying, "I don't understand."

"Never mind," said the man, with an ugly, awkward smile. "I've been taking this train for over twenty years now, ever since the end of the war. But up to now I've never met a Jew on this line. It's a very out-of-the-way line."

"Do I owe you an account of my movements?" asked Bruno angrily.

The stranger's head sank into his shoulders. "I didn't mean anything. Forgive me. I don't interfere in other people's business." In the adjacent compartments people were drinking heavily. A drunk stood in the doorway and sang bawdy songs. Although the windows were open, the smell of beer soaked the compartment. And the local words, whose taste Bruno knew so well, mingled with the smell of the beer.

To come home and sit next to a solid little Jew wearing a black skullcap whose whole being proclaimed self-satisfaction, grossness, and ugliness—in the worst of his dreams he could not have imagined such a thing possible. He was not comfortable with the lewd songs, but the Jew sitting next to him bothered him even more. If the compartment hadn't been so crowded he would have changed places. The Jewish businessman took out a prayer book and prayed.

"I didn't mean to offend you," he whispered.

"I understand," said Bruno. "I'm not angry with you."

"I'm glad," said the man, but the expression on his stolid face was annoyingly smug.

The train rushed through the countryside. Shadows flickered on the windows. No memories came to life in him. A dull, empty feeling gnawed at his insides. He tapped his fingers in time to the songs coming from the next compartment.

For years this journey had possessed his imagination, but everything, of course, had turned out differently. It seemed as if not he himself, but rather a kind of haste controlling him had brought him here. The journey home had no reality, except for the Jew sitting next to him, as ugly as sin. The Jew, sensing Bruno's suppressed hostility, huddled next to his medium-sized, cheap suitcase and closed the prayer book, as if he were afraid of the stranger's eye.

"Where are you from?" The Jew could not restrain his curiosity.

"Jerusalem," said Bruno shortly.

"What do you say." The Jew's mouth fell open, as if he had been caught in a lie, or even worse—cheating in business. "I'd never have believed it," he whispered. A foolish smile spread over his face and he said, "As for me, I'm sorry to say that I'm stuck here. Business is good. I haven't got the courage to abandon it. It's funny but that's the way it is. That's the way of the world, my friend."

Bruno did not respond.

The man continued. "What is a man? No better than an insect. He'll sell himself body and soul for a tasteless mess of pottage. My friends were better men than I. They chose labor." He said the last sentence clearly, choosing his words, and perhaps trying to force Bruno into a reaction. Bruno did not respond.

"I stayed behind. My wife wanted to stay here. I don't blame her. I didn't have the courage. There was one moment, in 1948, I remember it well. I said to my wife, 'I'm packing. We're going to Israel.' But something inside me, apparently, thought differently. I don't want to blame my wife. A man is nothing."

The train slowed down. The low houses of Stahl-heim peeped out of the green woods. The familiar shadows did not move him. The Jewish salesman folded his black coat, took hold of his cheap suitcase, and without saying, This is where I get off, he went and stood by the door. His figure softened, his suitcase merged into the faded partition. The incessant nervous haste pulsing in Bruno's temples now beat in his skull like a racing pump. The salesman seemed no longer to be a man but a lost shadow looking for a wall to cling to. Bruno wanted to reach out to him, but the Jew slipped away. Only when he got off the train and was standing on the platform did the Jewish salesman become real again: a giant insect spreading his limbs out in front of him. He stood still for a moment, then quickly wormed his way through the people on the platform and disappeared. The encounter with the salesman left Bruno sour and depressed.

The dining car was packed with people and here too a smell of beer hung heavily in the air. The waitress standing behind the counter laughed in a cracked voice. "See what he did to me and you don't care." She was apparently addressing her husband, but he had his head buried in the dark steam rising from a boiling pot.

The stations sped past, one after the other. The

plains disappeared. The train crossed the narrow ravine and climbed the plateau. Passengers thinned out, and the empty coaches swayed like drunkards. The man dozing in the next compartment woke and asked, "Are we far from Knospen?" His red, beer-soaked face split open, for a moment like a rotten watermelon. From now on the landscape changed to hilly pastures with spotted cows and heavy horses. The train came closer. The country cottages, rooted in this lush land for generations, were covered with red creepers. Bruno knew them like the scars on his body. The light grew gray and the train slowed. The green shadows came rushing in and the coach sank into a dull throbbing and stopped. "Knospen." At the sound of the conductor's voice the signal projecting at right angles from the pole dropped.

The station was empty. The shadow of the clock tower fell across the station square and cut it in two. Bruno dragged his suitcase along the platform and stood still. Now things began to grow more, if not absolutely, clear. His feet still throbbed with the swaying rhythm of the train. Paving stones lay side by side in the familiar pattern, but they seemed more worn. Even the warehouse door hung carelessly half open, as such sturdy old doors do. Only the voices were missing, and this gave the familiar scene a kind of cold clarity.

Bruno smiled, glad that his legs could still carry him. The dark green geranium pot was still there, looking as out of place and artificial as ever, a shoddy little piece of decor. "In any case, what difference does it make," he said, for some reason. Words deserted him, as did the fevered excitement; only weariness remained, a scaly armor. And suddenly he understood that there was no reason to hurry. He would have liked to peep into the warehouse and touch the ramshackle old door, but he suppressed this little desire because of another, which directed his feet toward the exit.

From the station to the town they had always taken a coach. Verdant country separated the station from the town. Here nature reigned, nourishing the provincial town with fruit and vegetables and especially with smells of the earth. For Bruno it was a mysterious place. He was glad that he did not have to subject himself to any emotional meetings. "An evening in the countryside," he said, repeating a phrase he had often heard in his childhood. "Nothing gladdens the heart like an evening in the countryside."

The engine hooted and the train set off. A few freight cars were left standing alone on the tracks. Bruno examined the dissolving shadow of the clock tower again. Dusk fell like a transparent curtain. Behind the station lay the village: green squares of meadows and orchards. The river, which also ran through the town, flowed here with a merry gurgling. Knospen loomed faintly in the distance, clasped in an embrace of greenery and oak trees.

The summer light, which lasted here until late, went on fading slowly. Next to the country inn stood a horse; a dog drowsed in the doorway. A country scene as banal as a cheap postcard. But for Bruno everything held a baffled, wondering question.

"Is there a bed for a stranger here?" he asked in the local dialect.

"With the greatest of pleasure," said the woman. "Was it on the evening train that the gentleman arrived?"

"On the local."

The simple, familiar words he had not used for years touched him like cold water. The inn was empty. The hard wooden floor gave way under his feet like a carpet. The room was large, overlooking the garden. A wide bed stood in the middle of the room, the walls were covered with pictures cut out of magazines, and on the table lay a corkscrew and a pocket knife with many different blades. The fading evening light glimmered in the corners.

"Business?" asked the woman, in the way of the locals, without undue ceremony.

"Of course."

"The singer's doing her turn tonight. There'll be fun and games."

"What's her name?" Bruno tried to keep the conversation going.

"The devil knows. She strips naked as the day she was born. The men can't get enough of her, young and old it's all the same."

She spoke to him simply, without affectation, as if to an habitué of the inn. She told him about some village hellion who had grabbed hold of the naked singer, dragged her out of the village hall, and led her through the streets. She swore shamelessly. And to Bruno it seemed it was not many years since he had left here, but a short holiday, a brief sleep—and now it was summer.

Outside, crowds were already besieging the village hall. The singer's carriage came gliding down the hill. Young men climbed onto balconies and telegraph poles and shouted in chorus, "Lilian, Lilian!" The carriage, harnessed to four beribboned horses, made its way through the crowd. The driver cracked his whip, but the crowd stood its ground.

The carriage came slowly to a stop at the entrance to the village hall. The driver climbed off his seat and plowed a way for her with his big hands. The young men shouted. The driver kept guard over the singer as if he were an animal tamer with a dancing bear. The singer alighted and the shouting merged into a great roar. *"Lilian!"* The driver closed the iron doors behind her.

But immediately a continuous howling went up, and stamping and whistles, as if they wanted to split the locked iron doors. In the meantime the back door was broken down and the crowd—men and boys—pushed through the breach. And the driver, seeing that he could not withstand the flood, shrugged his shoulders and opened the iron doors.

Darkness descended. Next to the kiosk a few children collected. At the entrance to the cinema the usher sat idly; in the beer cellar the old men quaffed their

beer from big tankards. Bruno tried to remember, but
no memories came. The first familiarity fell away from
him and a kind of chill, like a wet bandage, shrouded
his shoulders. He knew: everything here was familiar
and known, only a layer of moss had grown over the
walls. How clearly he saw the trees! He never saw trees
in his dreams, and yet how precisely they loomed up
before him, like a body of quivering light and shade:
the walnut tree next to the cinema, and the row of
chestnuts along the avenue.

"Why not take in a first show? There's a special
price," said the cinema usher.

"I'm too tired, worn out by the journey," said Bruno
as if apologizing to an old friend.

"That singer is driving everyone crazy, even the old
men," said the usher angrily and switched off the lights.
Apparently, the hall was empty.

The darkness thickened and Bruno remained in the
street. The walnut tree cast its shadow on the cobble-
stones and a damp wind blew from the hills. From
where he stood he could measure the circles of darkness rising up into the sky. How far is it from here
to Knospen?—quarter of an hour, no more. When he
was a boy, there had once been a heavy snowfall in
the spring. The family had returned from Vienna and
the carriage that should have been waiting for them at
the station had failed to arrive. And his father, in a
fur coat and a strange mood, had flung his arm out
toward the avenue and said, "How far is it from here
to Knospen?—quarter of an hour, no more." It wasn't
a real voice, only a kind of question in the air.

The familiar voice roused him from his weariness.
The voice grew dull, the memory slipped away. He
dragged himself back to the inn. The horse was tied
up in the stable, the dog was sleeping. The proprietress
stood in the doorway and said, "A very good evening
to you."

The small dining room, decorated with roses, struck
a note of cheap but cozy softness. The proprietress did
not offer him a menu but listed the dishes by their local

names. And all the time she kept on cursing the singer who was corrupting the youth. The two maids chattered loudly. Bruno watched their transparent maneuvers. Perhaps they expected a soft whistle, or an invitation, but since the invitation was not forthcoming, they chattered even more vivaciously. The proprietress asked him if he would like some music and Bruno nodded.

And when he went up to his room he could still hear the commotion coming from the village hall, a dying commotion. He took off his clothes and stretched out his legs. The rhythmic swaying that had accompanied him here took hold of him again. The only sight that came back to him was that big red head, soaked in beer and sausages, splitting open like a rotten watermelon.

2

THE meeting the next day was unemotional. He walked down the straight, narrow avenue with its two famous white shrines standing there like eternal resting places for the wayfarer. The sky was cloudless and the light poured calmly down. The acacia tree, growing wild outside the fence of the Hapsburg park, had not changed, neither in its height nor in the width of its trunk. It was in flower.

He walked on. For some reason he chose the shortcut he used to like when he was a schoolboy. Not far from his house he paused, as if he understood that he had gone too far. He took off his jacket and his eye rested on two tree stumps, standing side by side and chopped off at the same height to serve as seats. They were new, painted dark green. Drops of paint dribbled down their bark. That was the only change in this corner, and apart from it everything else was the same: the fence, the single iron chair.

Some schoolboys stood at the gymnasium gates. It was Tuesday, Bruno remembered, twelve o'clock. Latin was over for the day. Now everyone was in the sports hall. The two boys standing by the monument must have been excused on medical grounds. Still getting over a winter sickness, or perhaps they had suffered from rickets in their childhood.

He turned aside into the Old Bouquet of Flowers café. This was once the meeting place of the intellectuals who gathered here informally every summer to engage each other in stormy debates. Naturally, they were mainly Jews, dragging their restlessness behind them wherever they went. The café was now deserted. On the round tables stood blue vases of flowers spreading a greenish light. Two people stood at the back entrance arguing about an insurance policy. They spoke loudly. Bruno stood some distance from the window. Something at any rate had changed, he reflected. The slanting light, which had once crossed the floor, still crossed it and at the same angle, but the strip of light had grown much wider than before as the result of widening the back window. The floor did not seem to have changed at all. It was a parquet floor.

The air was full of apple blossom. The petals fell at the feet of two old men sitting in the avenue, sucking on their pipes. Buxom young women exposed their throats to the sun. In Brandenburg Park big dogs were running wild and fighting, but the gardener did not try to stop them. In his gymnasium days he would linger here on the way home from school. Brandenburg Park was never very grand. There was some wild broom climbing up the walls, and in the autumn the bare branches reflected a gentle melancholy. Here he would sometimes meet Hirzel, a working-class girl who did not last long at the gymnasium—because of the Latin and mathematics, but especially because of her father, a worn-out, obstinate farm laborer who would beat his wife and three daughters with the handle of a hoe. Even while she was still a pupil at the gymnasium her full, seething body was driving her wild, and when she left school they would sometimes see her in Brandenburg Park in the company of men smoking cigarettes.

He went back to stand at the gymnasium gates. There was no one now on the smooth marble steps. A blue-uniformed janitor walked up and down, his eyes glittering with the weariness and boredom of five o'clock in the afternoon. This was the hour, Bruno remembered, when they opened the reference library and the old Latin teacher gave a bibliography lesson there. Faces flitted past, but he did not recognize anyone. "The place hasn't changed, but the people evidently have," he said absentmindedly as if he were making small talk to himself with ready-made words.

And while he was standing there measuring the light, he discovered that the house opposite, the Rosenbergs' double-storied house, had grown a new creeper, wine red, and the attic window had been painted a dull green. The familiar sight flooded him with a stream of warmth. A second look, from close up, revealed that the height of the house had undergone a change too. They had added a roof, nicely covered with the creepers. And they had decorated the wall with a couple of rows of porcelain tiles.

Before his retirement Dr. Rosenberg had been the district veterinarian. Every day he and his wife would set out to take afternoon coffee at the Old Bouquet of Flowers. They were a tall couple and there was something severe in their bearing. They never spoke to anyone, and did not seem to have much to say to each other either. On the day before the deportation they hanged themselves against the wall, this wall now decorated with porcelain tiles. The whole day long they hung there and in the evening the fire brigade came to cut them down.

Bruno turned back to the park. His feet felt cold. This was the path the Rosenbergs had taken to the Old Bouquet of Flowers, walking in step, absorbed in their mute, private world. And when they reached their destination Dr. Rosenberg would lift his stick—a prearranged signal that they were ready for their coffee. More than their faces, he now remembered the way they walked. This stiff, measured tread now overtook his own feet too. He held on to the memory and said to himself, "He was once a veterinarian and then he retired, and against this wall, which has now been decorated with porcelain tiles, they put an end to their lives."

The night lights were already trembling on the signboard of the Henrietta bar. Dusk deepened. Bruno had apparently forgotten: at this season of the year the sky

changed almost hourly, and sometimes it was nothing
but the passage of the clouds, pausing over the town
for a moment and darkening it. They seemed to have
opened the bar early; the tables were already set. The
smell of beer-soaked wood greeted his nostrils. He bent
down and stood in the dark. "It's opening time," said
a voice from within. "Come in, please." It was a
feminine voice, not without a certain affectionate
familiarity. At once the girl appeared and held out her
hand as if greeting an unexpected guest. Bruno examined the gallery seats and the seats on floor level, and
turned to the girl with an indecisive look.

"I would suggest the table in the left-hand corner.
Reserved for the discriminating." Short, boyish, there
was no light or beauty in her face. She spoke in the
familiar accent and vocabulary of girls in her position.

"A stranger in these parts?" she asked.

"Yes."

"But you seem very regional."

Bruno, surprised by this new use of the word "regional," said, "From far away."

The girl expressed no surprise. She brought dark
beer and pretzels and said, "I hope you enjoy yourself
here. There's a new program—the Singapore Midgets.
Two cute little couples."

Bruno drank his beer and ordered more. "Where's
the singer?" he asked.

"I'm the singer," said the girl. "I do a bit of singing
in the intervals. I composed a song for the midgets."

Words he had not used for years rose to the tip of
his tongue and he was glad to have them back again.

The bar filled with people. Whispered voices filled
the place together with the smell and rustle of new
clothes.

"I came on the train and here I am," he said to himself absentmindedly.

The singers emerged from behind the curtain. They
were four swarthy midgets wearing blue uniforms. They
took up their places on the stage. The dim light dwarfed
them even more. The saxophone let out a long wail and

the dwarfs came together and stamped their feet in time to the music. "Aren't they cute?" asked the hostess. The wailing of the saxophone grew louder and the tempo increased. The midgets separated and scattered, singing as they went; a little spotlight pursued them. It was now apparent that the bar was larger than it appeared from the front entrance. The corners were full.

"Forgive me, but haven't I met you before?"

"No, that's not possible."

"But I'm sure, once at least. Or maybe I'm mistaken."

Bruno laughed and said, "I left here many years ago."

"In that case, I must be mistaken," she said and covered her face with her hands. "I'm always making mistakes."

"We all make mistakes." Bruno tried to make light of her confusion.

"But I'm an expert at it." There was something charming about her candor.

"Where are you from?" She tried again.

"From Jerusalem. Does that mean anything to you?"

"Just a minute," said the girl. "Just a minute. It rings a bell. You must be, how shall I put it . . ."

"Quite simply—a Jew."

The girl stared, openmouthed, and said, "I knew it." Her high-pitched laughter broke into splinters in her mouth.

"What did you know?"

"I sensed it," she said and took his hand. "Me too, how shall I say it, my granny was Jewish, her name was Regina. Wouldn't you like to spend the night with me somewhere else?"

"With pleasure."

"Two more songs and I can go. The midgets are overexcited tonight. We'll let them finish their turn first. The proprietor gave them too much to drink. Last night they were very lazy. He squeezes everything he can out of them."

The midgets went wild. The spectators roared with laughter and showered them with sweets and coins. In the end they climbed the rafters and hung from the roof singing suggestive songs.

"Amazing how quickly they picked up German."

"How long have you been working here?"

"I think it must be six years by now. I never went to high school. My father thought I wasn't suited to it. The truth is that I never tried very hard. Do you think that's a bad thing?"

The wild, pounding beat came to an end. The girl skipped onto the stage and sang a song about love and roses. The dwarfs slid from the rafters and huddled in a corner panting heavily. The proprietor gave them drinks with straws and they sat sucking solemnly, wiping the sweat from their little foreheads.

The first show was over. The girl put on her tight-fitting coat and turned toward the door. Bruno was already dull with drink. The alcohol fumes were clouding his brain. The night was fresh and apple blossoms fell lightly as snowflakes. Nothing has changed, he reflected, even the trees still slant slightly to the south.

"Where are you staying?"

"At the railway station, in the Merry Horse."

"That's a long way off. I haven't got a room of my own any more. I'm saving. Rooms cost entirely too much lately, and I need a room with a separate entrance. Too bad I don't have my own room tonight. I like people with Jewish blood."

"In what way are they different from anyone else?"

"I don't know. Pure Austrians are crude. Don't you think so?"

"Are there many part-Jews here?"

"A few. A month ago I discovered one. A young boy, very withdrawn. He drank a lot of brandy and when he saw the midgets putting on their act he went crazy and hit the proprietor. It was a real scandal— he didn't look Jewish, but I knew. No real Austrian would drink the way he drank. Over the years you learn to tell them apart. Where shall we go then?"

"Wherever you like."

"If it's up to me, I'd like to go for a walk by the river. I haven't been for a walk by the riverside for ages. At school they used to call them nature walks, didn't they? Or maybe I'm wrong? Correct me if I'm wrong."

"And since then?"

"I haven't been for any walks since then. The men here aren't nature lovers."

"And don't people come here for holidays?"

"Not very often. Apart from our bar there's nothing to attract them. You said Jerusalem, didn't you? As far as I know it's called the Holy City, isn't it? Correct me if I'm wrong. I was never much good at history."

"Yes, you're quite right."

"My Granny Regina used to say that Jews are good to their fellow men. I inherited this ring from her. By the way, what's your name?"

"Bruno."

"Mine's Brunhilda. People who like me call me Hill. Isn't the river pretty at night? My Granny Regina was a very wealthy woman. All the Jews are rich—correct me if I'm wrong. My father used to say that we mustn't boast about Granny's money. But money's not a disgrace, is it? Correct me if I'm wrong."

"You're quite right."

"I'm glad. But why do you look so sad?"

"I'm tired," said Bruno, and put out his arm to embrace her. Hill snuggled into his coat and kissed his neck.

"All part-Jews are sad, but I like them. My Granny Regina was an exceptional woman. She used to say that people should broaden their horizons. In our house nobody used words like that. My father used to say that Granny Regina had words of her own. Forgive me."

"What for?"

"For not having a room of my own."

"It doesn't matter. We'll go for a walk."

"I'd like to thank you."

"What for?"

Bruno knew them well: stupidity, innocence, and cunning all wrapped up in one feminine bundle.

"I didn't understand," said Hill. "Did you come for a visit?"

"In a way. I was born here."

"What a pleasant surprise."

She didn't understand the first thing about it. She held out her hands as if she wanted to take hold of a familiar object slipping out of her grasp. She smoothed her dress down and said, "I suppose you'll find a lot of old acquaintances. Isn't that exciting?"

"I'm a Jew," said Bruno, rather artificially.

"In that case you must be a rich man; I expect you've visited lots of countries."

"All over the world." Bruno laughed.

"How wonderful. I know, the Jews are always successful. They're so clever."

Boats glided down the river and the night was cloudless over the open meadows. Hill burrowed into his coat and snuggled against him—too demonstrative, like all her kind. Nevertheless, he felt an unfamiliar emotion spreading through him.

"I'd like you to meet my sister, Eveline. She went to the gymnasium for two years. She has a diploma." It was obvious that contact with this stranger embarrassed her a little. She was seeking some kind of support outside herself, in her elder sister.

It was already after midnight. Hill still had one last little duty to perform at the bar, a midnight song. She apologized and said that from now on she would not accept any obligations at so late an hour. They went back by a shortcut, through the famous rose garden.

On the illuminated stage the midget couples were stamping their feet to the beat of the saxophone. Their faces were red with strain. "You didn't get anything from me tonight. But I'm going to keep a nice evening especially for you. You're not cross, are you?"

"No. Tonight was a nice evening."

"I'm glad." Once more she clung to the words she knew.

He knew she did not have many words, and she used the same ones with everyone; and as he was putting his hand into his pocket, to pay her, Hill slipped away into the passage. She waved her right hand in a gesture unfamiliar to him—as if saying "There's no need." Bruno stood still and said, "Until tomorrow."

His legs were giving way under him from weariness but his mind was clear and unclouded. He stood next to the shrine for a moment and crossed the narrow avenue, and without feeling the distance, he found himself standing at the inn.

"Did you enjoy yourself?" asked the proprietress in the local dialect.

"Very much."

"I'm glad to hear it. Over here the lads hung around in the street all night long. There were two windows smashed in the cinema. And a crush in the village hall you wouldn't believe—all for the sake of that whorish singer. You were quite right to go to town. In town, at least, there's a bit of culture."

3

THE next morning spring sunshine flooded the broad streets. The tall trees cast their damp shadows over the hedges and the morning lay cool and quiet on the walls of the houses. Two days here already. The same light and the same shade, falling from one house to the other straight and sharp as a ruler. Even the old roofs covered in green ivy stuck up at the same blunt angle. Only at the bottom of the gates was there a new, light mist. Apart from this there was no change; not a single tree had been uprooted from its place. Even the old stone posts marking the old boundaries still stood in their places. Except for the light, for the cold reality, it would have been like a vivid dream with all its details painted in carefully and precisely, but the cold reality was clear and decisive: you're here, Bruno, you're here.

Next to the bakery stood two old women. The fresh bread in their hands gave off a fragrant, familiar peace. "They haven't taken the poppy-seed rolls out of the oven yet." Bruno heard this sentence clearly, as if the words filtered toward him through a heavy curtain of water. "They came late today. The baker got drunk last night." The answer too came through clearly. The old ladies turned off into the lane, dragging their thin shadows with them. There was no movement, only a kind of clarity of light and shade, just as it had been, many years ago.

Still fascinated by the tiny, precise shadows, he saw
a man standing at the crossroads, stooping slightly,
leaning on a cane. At first the man looked momentarily
sunk in thought, and then it became clear that he had
no intention of moving. Bruno approached. The way
the man was standing, rooted to the spot, stirred no
memory in his mind, and he was about to turn aside,
to the south where the lights of the morning were
spreading in two broad arcs, and so he did—when
suddenly he realized: Brum, it was Brum.

The man turned his back to Bruno and the shadow
next to him changed its angle slightly with him. Bruno
moved a step forward. There was no doubt: it was he.
The broad forehead, the eyebrows, the moustache
spreading from one side of his face to the other. Even
the high boots exposed by the slit in his buttoned-up
coat.

In the bitter days of the last year, before the deportation—in the terrible confusion when people were
exchanging their religion, selling their shops, abandon-
ing beloved wives, taking drugs like alcohol—in those
bitter days, Brum had married his housemaid. Within
a few weeks the miracle had taken place: Brum the
thin, Brum the ascetic, was metamorphosed into a
different kind of Brum. He grew taller, his shoulders
filled out, and a luxuriant moustache appeared on his
face; he sat with his new wife in the cellar of the White
Horse drinking beer. He, who had never uttered a
word, spoke to her at the top of his voice, as if she
were deaf. Even in those bitter days their appearance
in the streets of the town caused a stir. Bruno's father
said, "Would you believe it?" Every day they would
pass by the window, proceeding slowly and steadily
toward the cellar, that fountainhead of beer. Who
would have imagined that he of all people, this man of
delicate and morbid sensibilities, this bachelor of so
many years' standing, would achieve the impossible?
Would be reincarnated in his own lifetime into the like-
ness of an Austrian cattle farmer, completely erasing

all the soft, delicate lines of his former self? But he did it, and he did it to perfection. And afterward too, when things went from bad to worse, when cheap music and vile intentions ran riot in the streets, even then he would set out every day for the White Horse, walking with a sure and steady step; as though his former self had never existed. Strange—no one tried to stop them as they walked down the street. Everyone, it seemed, understood that the old Brum was dead. The new one wasn't Brum any more.

"Mr. Brum." Bruno's whisper grew louder. The man turned the upper part of his body slightly, fixed him with a stare, and said, "You are mistaken, sir." The stare fixed Bruno's face for a moment and then dropped. Bruno twisted his face into an apology, bowed, and turned away. He felt a biting cold in his fingers, as if stung by night frost. Still, he dared to turn his head. The man stood there, tilted at the same angle. But now it seemed that he was about to bend over. He shifted his stick slightly and moved almost imperceptibly from one circle of shade to another.

Bruno entered the Old Bouquet of Flowers next to the crossroads without thinking. Brum's resounding voice had held him for a moment, trapped with no way out, and he had gone into the café seeking refuge. Here was the silence found only in old wooden buildings. For some reason he took off his hat, and the aroma of coffee fortified with chicory flooded his nostrils.

Every Tuesday in the early hours of the afternoon he used to come here with his mother. It would be after the interminable Latin lesson when his head was clenched like a fist. These unforgotten little outings were usually uneventful, but they left behind a train of sweetness that would seep into his sleep together with the smell of chicory. On Tuesday afternoons the customers were mainly pensioners, each sunk in his own proud loneliness; but the place had a charm all its own due to the proprietress, Lonka—Lonka and her

Slavic accent so full of vitality amid the dry formality of the Austrian petite bourgeoisie.

"Does the boy drink coffee yet?" Lonka would ask. "Coffee with lots of milk," Mother would say softly. And Lonka would take his head in both her hands and say, "A wonderfully Jewish face. The kind of face I love." "Why expose the child's disgrace in public?" Mother would whisper with a wink. "Madame," Lonka would say, "Jews are the finest people in the world. I grew up among Jewish students, you know." And Mother would respond, joining in the spirit of the thing, "In that case, Lonka, I must bow to your superior knowledge." And Lonka would say, "My lust for Jews, Madame, knows no bounds."

He opened his eyes and was glad to see that nothing had changed. The big front window, full of blue flowers, looked modest and natural, as it always had. The aromatic steam of the coffee hung almost imperceptibly in the air. In this café, as in all old-fashioned cafés, some of the corners were brightly lit and some were dim and shadowy. By the front window adorned with its blue garden flowers he would sit with his mother for hours, listening to music.

While he stood there wondering, an old woman appeared and raised her voice as if she were deaf. "What can we do for the gentleman?" It was Lonka. All that was left of her mane of brown hair was a wispy down of gray. Her ears were exposed; the heavy words sticking in her throat seemed about to break out of her mouth.

"Coffee with chicory, please," said Bruno.

"With pleasure," said the old woman and dragged her feet toward the steaming kitchen. There was nobody else in the café at this hour of the morning. The spring light poured in abundantly; in the back his father used to sit with Uncle Salo, arguing or in silence; those dark recesses belonged to his secret anxieties; the wide front window bordered with blue flowers was the secret between him and his mother.

"Coffee with chicory," muttered the old lady, carrying the tray in her trembling hands like the old ladies who carried icons to the shrine.

In those days, so far off but so clear, Lonka had been young and strong, her head wild with its tangled mane of hair. Her eyes shone with the sauciness of a barmaid brought up in a bar. And when visitors came from Prague her youth would break out in a full blossoming of freedom. Austrians were of no account in her eyes. Her husband, who was an Austrian, had seduced her into coming here. She had never forgiven him.

On Sundays, when her husband went out to meet the friends of his youth—farmers and factory hands—in the country inns next to the river, she would allow herself a certain freedom. She would sit with the students and tell them about student life in Prague. Her father kept an inn next to the university and the students would have wild times there until late at night. There she had picked up a number of words that she was fond of using. Her husband could not endure her memories; he would say dismissively, "Those miserable Prague memories." In such a moment of freedom she confessed to Bruno's mother that if she hadn't been seduced by that Austrian, in other words her husband, she would have married a Jew. About the Jews she would speak secretly, with a sly expression on her face.

When he was still a child, during one of the cold winters, Lonka had had too much to drink, and with gestures full of freedom she had proclaimed, "Long live the Czechoslovakian Republic! Hats off to the Jewish students who make secret love to the girls of Czechoslovakia!"

There was an uproar. Her brother-in-law, her husband's brother, tried to tie up her hands, but she was so drunk that she went on shouting from behind the locked lavatory door. It was a nasty business. Bruno's mother tried to intervene, but the brother-in-law raised his voice, tied the door handle with a rope, and swore that he would never let her out. Ever since that incident a great change had come over Lonka's face. Her appearances became less frequent and her husband, who stood next to the till, introduced a loud, vulgar tone that changed the atmosphere of the café.

"Another cup?" the old lady asked loudly.

"Yes, please."

4

TWO days here already. The brightness in the air is too much for his eyes to bear. Therefore he does not venture far. He sits in the center of town, but in the center too everything stands in its place, utterly familiar. Once there were no nightclubs here, only cafés or pubs. His classmates would go down to the southern neighborhoods to hunt their first prey—country girls. The next day they would come to school with an arrogant gleam in their eyes and hostility to Jews in their hearts. In the religious instruction classes, which took place twice a week, their questions would embarrass the priest until he would exclaim, "Degenerates!"

Once or twice they tried to drag him with them. But because the invitations were malicious and full of ill will, Bruno ignored the dirty nocturnal meetings near the railway station. For this he was, of course, taunted, and earned the title "sissy Jew." They were bigger but he was quicker on his feet, and in gym he excelled at climbing the rope ladders.

These little details, which had not come into his mind for years, now broke out of their hiding places. They were no longer forgotten but living, breathing feelings. In the last, bitter months when he had been expelled from the gymnasium and they were gathering in the youth club yard wearing brown uniforms, he would sit for hours in his room, struggling with difficult Latin texts. The confusion was terrible but his mother would not relent: man is not an animal, after all. And thus, while everything around them warned of the approaching earthquake he was tied to algebra exercises, to analyzing complicated Latin sentences. It was his mother's wish.

He stood up. For a moment he thought of making himself known to Lonka, but straight away he realized: Lonka was very old. Why upset her at her age? "The coffee was excellent," he said. "I'm glad," she said, and went into the kitchen without giving him another glance.

The April light now poured straight down from the sky and flooded the streets. The white blossoms filled the air with a cool, subtle scent. Again he saw Brum, the thick moustache covering his cheeks, the clean-shaven chin. Apparently his walk was already over. He was sitting on a bench. Now there was no doubt in his mind that the man was Brum. But how could he be reached? Brum, he was about to plead. My name is Bruno A. I'm the son of the writer A. May I have a word with you? You seem to be the only person here who knows me. I feel overwhelmed by this flood of familiar sights.

Brum sat on the bench, his chin resting on his stick. His glance was direct, still, unmoved, but his boots said more; there was something of the dejection of old age about them.

Bruno turned aside. The low houses, lovingly tended, were modest and unassuming. A provincial calm rested on their roofs. They were exactly as he remembered them. The years had come and gone and they had not changed. Only the vividness was new. This strange homecoming had not been his idea. Something else had brought him here, something of a practical nature, so to speak.

In 1965 he had received two letters from two well-known publishers, informing him of a revival of interest in his father's work. This news, from far-off, forgotten places, had not made him happy. He was in the process of separating from his wife. It was a long, painful separation, a separation with many reasons but no single defined reason. For a few months he vacillated

between his old pain and the new, dark hope; and with
no other way out he asked for leave, packed his suitcases and set out for Vienna, and from Vienna here.

Coming back had not been his idea. Something
stubborn and abiding inside him had sealed off whole
sectors of his emotions. In the course of the years he
had learned to live without them, as a person learns
to live with a paralyzed limb. The two letters suddenly
coming from far away had stirred the old scar into a
new pain: his father. His father. The disgrace he had
not dared to touch, seething silently all these years
like pus inside a wound. They said he had died half-
mad in Theresienstadt, and that before he died he had
tried to convert to Christianity. Another rumor said
that he had not been sent to Theresienstadt but to
somewhere near Minsk, where he had been seen a
number of times in the slaughterhouse. And that was
not the end of the rumors. Almost every year some
broken echo had reached him and reopened his hidden
wound. His disgrace had many faces: contempt, hatred,
deliberate forgetfulness. He gave his father no credit
at all. But in recent years, perhaps because he himself
was already approaching his father's age, he felt the
old, wretched shame swelling inside him in a different
way, no longer hatred but a kind of distance and even
wonder.

Now he stood in the place where he had once stood
with his father. Now he had reached his father's age,
perhaps even a few years more. And like his father's,
his own marriage was not happy. He had come back
to his first place and there was no one left there close
to him. So he stood and stared at this strange creature
called Brum. In all probability, the old man himself
did not remember that his name was Brum, but he,
Bruno, remembered that his name was Brum.

Brum rose to his feet, tapped his stick on the pavement, and turned toward the cattle path, which was
fenced in on either side by a low wall. The path broke
off abruptly and stray sunbeams lit up the corner of the

park behind the pharmacy, revealing yellow stains on the wall beneath the triangular roof. It seemed to Bruno now that he knew this corner very well. Here he and his jolly Uncle Salo would pause for a moment, his uncle to glance at the newspaper and he to lick an ice cream. It was always just for a moment, but precisely this fleeting moment—of a child's concentration on the full taste and flavor of the ice cream—had registered clearly, perhaps because it was nothing but a simple, sensuous pleasure.

He passed from tree to tree without venturing too far afield. There were many familiar places here whose names he no longer remembered. His feet felt heavy, weighted down. In vain he tried to remember, and since no memories came he dragged himself from tree to tree and bench to bench. The afternoon passed and in the corners of the park the dusk gathered.

At nightfall he went back to the singer Hill's den. Hill wasn't there. She had caught a cold, they said. The place was full, but not crowded. The midgets sat on the counter and sang sad, exotic songs. They looked like old men whose faces had been shrivelled small with sorrow. A young Japanese, who was sitting nearby and had apparently had too much to drink, opened his heart. He too, it seemed, had hoped to find Hill and had drunk too much while he waited.

For two years now he had been a student at the technical college near Knospen. On a grant. But homesickness for Japan was driving him crazy; it made it hard for him to study. Hard to excel. He didn't like the food. He drank a lot. In Japan, even though it was a modern country, there were still corners of natural beauty and happiness. A man was born and died without having any say in the matter, but the little, deceptive freedom in between was what gave meaning to this life and the one after it. Now he was stuck here, in this Austrian wasteland containing nothing but beer and sounds neither shapely nor subtle.

He spoke German mixed with English words. There

was a strange melody in his voice, which for some reason pleased Bruno's tired ears. The midgets went on singing, but the Japanese took no notice of them. They came from Asia, true, but their music was not genuine—they were slaves to a corporation. Bruno drank too. The drink dulled his senses, but his mind, as if to spite him, stayed clear. The clear April days had left their clarity in his mind. It was hard for him to rid himself of it.

The drunken Japanese student kept on trying to convince him that in Japan life was still real; the Americans had destroyed a lot, but not the living tissue.

"Where are you from?" he suddenly asked suspiciously. "Are you a native of this place?"

"From Jerusalem," said Bruno.

"This is truly a night of wonders," cried the Japanese. "Here I am sitting and thinking about my little village in Japan when up comes some stranger and tries to make a fool of me by saying he's from the Holy Land."

"From Jerusalem," repeated Bruno and held out his passport.

"There's no doubt about it, someone's trying to get through to me tonight." The Japanese dropped his head. "At first I thought I was surrounded by hostile spirits here, and now you come along and say you're from Jerusalem. The Holy City. Do you believe?"

"I believe."

"You are my brother. My brother. In this exile. God never set foot in this place. The evil spirits like beer, it seems. They find the Austrian beer to their taste. All night I've been sitting here and thinking: What does God want of me? What does he want me to do now, in this strange town, in this insane bar, among these people who are strangers to me? If he brought me here, there must be some purpose in it. Otherwise I would never have landed here. You come from Jerusalem and you must know what I mean. What did they tell you there? Tell me."

"They told me nothing," said Bruno.

"That's impossible," said the Japanese. "I come from Japan and you come from Jerusalem. Did we come here for no purpose? We were meant to meet."

"Perhaps," said Bruno.

"Is there any doubt in your mind?"

"No," said Bruno. "I'm trying to understand."

"We should have met years ago. Because we've met once before. Do you believe in reincarnation?"

"I'm trying to understand."

"It's a great faith, a true faith."

Bruno stood up and said, "I know someone. His name was Brum. A tall, thin man who hardly opened his mouth, and he was suddenly changed into somebody else. Now he doesn't answer to his name. I call him and he doesn't answer to his name."

"Of course," said the Japanese. "He's been changed into someone else. He can't answer. He doesn't remember."

Bruno tried to overcome his giddiness and remain on his feet. "I have to go."

"But my friend," said the Japanese, "we mustn't miss this opportunity. Who knows when we'll meet again?"

"I promise you," said Bruno, "that we will meet again."

The Japanese looked at him sadly and said, "How rare such meetings are. And when they do take place they're so soon over. And the darkness comes again. What am I doing here in this lousy Austria?"

Bruno shook off the spell cast by the Japanese and left.

The night was full. A delicate scent of acacias mingled with sawdust rose from the gardens and courtyards. There were a few fishing boats on the river and the solitary voices rising from the water intensified the silence. In the last spring, or maybe the one before the last, he remembered, Aunt Theresa stood by this tree and spoke strangely about the terrible sufferings of

Jesus. His father, who hated all cults, and especially Christian ceremonial, had made some offensive remark. Theresa had not responded. They walked a while in silence: suddenly Theresa started weeping bitterly. His mother, who had not interfered in the argument, went up to her sister, took her head in her hands and said in a voice full of tenderness, "What do you want of them? They don't understand." Afterward they walked down the avenue without speaking. His mother and Theresa walked ahead, and a short distance behind them, he and his father, as if in the aftermath of some searing pain.

And while the memory flooded him he saw a man standing behind the shrine. For a moment it seemed as if the man was looking for a way out, but when he heard footsteps approaching, he crouched back against the wall. He made a careless movement, however, and revealed his face. It was Brum, Brum in a different posture—dwarfed, as if he had sunk lower to the ground since their first meeting. Bruno stopped and the following words escaped his mouth: "Why are you running away from me?" His voice hung frozen in the air. Bruno continued. "I'm Bruno A., the son of A. the writer. I remember you. You used to come to our house. Don't you want to see me?"

Brum's shadow emerged for a moment from the portico of the shrine, stretched out, and without a sound spread two shadow arms, which for some reason looked like visors of a cap projecting from his head on the ground. Bruno went on, "I've been here for two days already. I don't know anybody here. I went to Lonka's café. She's aged a lot. Don't you remember me, Brum? You used to bring me chocolate-coated nuts."

Brum raised his stick with a strange, theatrical gesture. He bundled a few incongruous sentences together—a jumble of vulgarities and pompous phrases—and flung them into the empty air.

"What do you want? I don't understand you—" Bruno asked, as one might question an oracle.

"I hate you." Brum thrust at him.

"I won't tell anyone, it'll be just between us two." Bruno clung to him despairingly.

Brum, apparently astounded by Bruno's intentions, raised his stick and said, "Don't dare come near me. I will strike you."

5

A WEEK already gone in this familiar exile and
nothing done. Most of the day he spends sitting on a
bench measuring the shadows of the church spires;
realizing again that nothing has changed here, only
him—he is already his father's age.

And when he tires of measuring the shadows, he
strolls along Hapsburg Avenue, and here too nothing
has changed. As if the scenes of his childhood have
been embalmed in all their subtlest nuances of light
and shade, from the awnings above to the paving stones
below. And between them the moist breezes of spring
rising from the river and mingling with the scent of
apple blossoms. Even the Jewish shops have preserved
their outward appearance, like the Lauffers' drapery
shop. None of them have survived but their shop is
still standing at exactly the same angle as before, perfectly preserved, even the geraniums in their pots. Now
a different man is sitting there with a different woman.
Strange—they don't look like murderers.

His recollection of Lauffer's wife was vague, but
Lauffer himself he remembered vividly. On that last,
terrible night in the locked temple, Lauffer had crawled
on all fours to the ark, to the rabbi. His narrow face
had assumed the terrible features of a wounded animal;
he crawled along cursing the rabbi without pause—
because of him this evil had come upon the people.
But for him, for his sermons, his nagging and demands
for money and activity, no one would have known who

was a Jew. What was he but an informer? The rabbi pleaded as with a bandit but Lauffer would not let him be. Now everything stands there without them, comfortable and homely, bathed in the same familiar light returning every year in its placid provincial rhythm. Here and there he spots a few elegant cripples, bearing their wounds with cold pride, but they too are steeped in the serenity of the little town living its life to the sounds of the seasons. And when he leaves the center, the green horizons open out before him and he forgets for a moment that he is here, in his town, in the midst of the strangers who fill its every corner. This was where they used to come for nature lessons when he was a child, to observe the birds and learn to recognize the wild flowers. The nun, her face sealed up in a white wimple, would point a long finger and say, "This, children, is a pansy." It seems to him that this white finger, straight and probing, is still standing at the same sharp angle as when it had first been brandished at him.

Years later, when he had reached the first level at the gymnasium and was lashed to the yoke—Latin and algebra exercises—he would come here with his mother. They would pause and stand still for a long time. His mother's face would slip into a deep meditation. And to him the moment would seem like an act of religious submission; and a sudden fear, which he had never expressed in words, would fill him with dread. It was only the blue light, of course, pouring over the arched entrance to the town. But he, for some reason, was always filled with fear by this blue torrent and by his mother's humble face.

And afterward a long shadow would follow them all the way home, where the heavy front door would chop it off and leave it outside. And sometimes at night when he was in his bed, the amputated shadow would creep up the wall and fawn on the window and invade his sleep with a tender pain. That's what it was like in spring. Or to be more precise—the beginning of spring. The world would suddenly emerge in a

spectrum of brilliant colors. Every day had its own
little joys, every day its own imperceptible partings.
Even then death was hiding in the house. A polite, discreet death, whose manifestations could only be sensed
in the sad melting of the sunsets.

And while he stood spellbound in the familiar
strangeness he saw a woman approaching. She looked
old and very fat—her feet falling heavily on the pavement; but suddenly he saw that she was wearing a
beret. An elderly woman would never wear a beret
unless she had once studied in a teachers' seminary or
served in a convent—only a woman who had spent
some time in one of these two places would go on
wearing a beret when she grew old. And when she
came close and he stood facing her he felt a warm
breath caress his neck. "Louise"—the name broke out
of him. The old woman was startled. She fell back a
step or two and seemed about to dismiss him with a
scornful look, but he seized hold of her arm like a
hunter falling on his prey. "Louise, don't you know
me? I'm Bruno . . ." He was startled at the sound of
his own voice.

"No."

He bowed his head before her in despair.

She turned her head away like a person pushed into
a corner, looking for help from some other quarter.
But then she turned it back again, stared at him, and
said, "You said 'Bruno,' didn't you?"

"Yes."

"Ah! You are Bruno."

"Louise, you remember." He wrung his hands.

Louise. The tender touch of female things and the
tiny footsteps of a country girl taking her first steps on
a parquet floor. He still remembered her arrival, the
way she stood embarrassed in the doorway and the
smell of the woods she brought with her from her village. Small and slender, her head bound in a bright
peasant kerchief, as if she came trailing the green
meadows of her village behind her. Even her name bore
the sweet magic of shy, slender girls. The first nights

after her arrival, when his parents went out to concerts, Louise would sit by his side and tell him about her village. Her voice had the deep, throaty sound of open country. It seemed that her village was situated on a mountain slope with a river flowing at its foot, a strong river that drowned at least one man a year in its spring torrents—for in the springtime the river was full. He still remembered the look on her face when she told him this. She was herself like the mountain slope from which she had been uprooted. And so, through her, the tranquility of remote villages entered his sleep. Frank, open, like Louise's face. Sometimes the stories would go on until late at night. For the first time he was initiated into the lore of stableboys, fights over land leases, shoeing horses, well-ploughed land and good harvests, and floods that swept earth and terraces away. She spoke of these things with an even, unbroken flow of words, in the way he imagined that peasants must speak, without undue emotion. Her quiet voice was as gentle as water welling of its own accord.

In the course of time the nights with Louise grew longer. The squabbling in her village had a darker side: ill will, treachery, and grim acts of vengeance. For the first time he saw that her innocence was not pure innocence, perhaps because he himself had changed.

But the magic was not spoiled. It went on and on, like chapters in a fairy tale. When he was ten years old his parents took a trip, in the long school vacation, and he was left alone with Louise for the first time. They slept in the salon, she on the couch and he in the folding Morris chair. Now she asked many questions. She knew something about Jews but not much. The tales they told in her village were full of fear and wonder: a certain young girl who was seduced by a Jew, an artist. First she ran away to Vienna and from there to America. For years they heard nothing. Then they received a postcard saying that she had changed her religion and was no longer a Catholic. Her father, a wealthy farmer, took the bitter news like a rock. From then on, said Louise, Jews were regarded among them as bold seducers, and the young girls were warned against them. When she said this she laughed. Her laughter among the cushions sounded different, perhaps because her voice had been tempered by the whispers she had absorbed in our house.

Between one concert and the next, which his parents always attended, came the short vacations. He would stay at home with Louise, nestled in her pillows or playing lotto on the floor. Then he saw for certain that something had changed in her. She was prettier and her hair was longer, but the frank, open look that had reflected the waters of her native river had dulled. She would ask, "What do the Jews believe in? Do they believe in Jesus too, and his blessed Mother?" Her questions confused him. In his embarrassment he would laugh and say, "They love the devil, too." And she would stare at him in her peasant stupor and say nothing. But the secret did not lose its power. It was in Louise's very being, her hips, her feet shuffling on the parquet floor. But above all it was her mouth, her fine teeth, her sensuous, delicately pursed lips—all joined in the melody of her laughter. Sometimes he would wake up and find himself locked in her arms. At the time, she still slept in the nightdress she had brought with her from her village, a nightdress made of linen. The smell of the linen and the smell of her body scented with a cheap eau de cologne would rob his sleep of the little weight it possessed and turn it into a floating doze. He did not tell this secret to anyone. When his parents returned, the delicate web would be destroyed. Louise would retire to the kitchen and he to his exercise books—until the next concert came around.

Sometimes they would go for walks. Louise would say, "You're spoiled, aren't you?"

"Why?"

"In the country, boys of your age are already working."

"Where do they work?"

"They help their parents in the fields."

"Will you take me to the village?"

"What's there to see in the village?" she said and laughed.

In the third year of her service with them it was spring and his parents set out on their short vacation. As soon as they left, the sweet silence crept out of its hiding place. And while he stood listening to the murmurs of the empty house a tall young man with the look of a waiter at a summer resort appeared in the doorway. He stared at Louise and she blushed. He came every evening and stayed late. Sometimes he would join in their games of lotto and humming a waltz to himself he would say, "The boy has a head on his shoulders. A Jewish head. You'll never cheat him."

And so for the first time he tasted the bitterness of betrayal. He did not know yet that it was a betrayal, but his hands knew it. One night he noticed that Louise was wearing a pink nightdress with two roses embroidered on its bodice. When Bruno asked her she said that the young man had given it to her as a gift. His feeling of betrayal was accompanied by an ugly pain.

The grim days of 1937 came, the holidays grew less frequent, and when they did go away they took him with them. Their quarrels were bitter. Not a day passed without a quarrel. And at night when he sat over his books, copying and doing exercises, Louise would put on her new clothes and go out to enjoy herself. He heard her coming home in his sleep, locking and barring the outside door. She apparently got herself into trouble. His mother sent her to an out-of-town doctor. She began to lose her country looks. She would vow never to give her body to seducers again. But she did not keep her vow. There was another accident, and Louise's face after it was discovered took on shame, innocence, and cunning all mixed up together. After every visit to the doctor her face grew more refined and lines of sadness spread over her forehead. And as one accident followed another she lost her country expressions and grew more like Bruno's family every day, even in her accent. His mother gave her clothes. Some-

times she looked like a young student, her face drawn
by her attempts to study. The young uncles who fre-
quented their house said that Louise had grown very
pretty of late. For some reason, these remarks, whose
true meaning evaded him, grieved Bruno.

And in the last, bitter year, full of confusion, when
the house became unbearable, she too could not make
up her mind between her men friends and a secretarial
course. Her hesitation did not last long though. One
day she stole their winter clothes and jewelry and ran
away. The bitter days that came then effaced her
memory and in the course of the years her name disappeared completely from his mind.

They went into the first café. She was short and fat.
But for the beret he would not have recognized
Louise—the beret was the last remnant of her charm.
She herself was a round barrel collapsing under the
weight of her obesity. Her upper lip was thicker than
her lower one and she pronounced the name Bruno
like a peasant. And added "Thank the Lord" for good
measure, like a woman who went to church on Sundays.

She said, "I can't believe my eyes."

"For a week now . . ." said Bruno, and left the
sentence unfinished.

It was a little eat-and-run place with no dignity, a
transistor playing raucously and continuously on the
shelf. A few laborers sat by the counter drinking beer.
Two old men played dominoes. The kettle on the table
radiated heavy tedium. Now he saw from close up: her
hair was sparse, her temples ploughed into deep fur-
rows. There was a flat scar on her nose and two protruding veins. "I was married twice but it didn't work
out. One son in Vienna and one in Frankfurt," she
summed up shortly. He tried to discover a familiar
feature. In her eyes there was nothing. Little eyes sunk
in pale fat. About her son in Vienna she said, "He
works in a bar and earns a decent living." Now he
knew for sure: of Louise nothing remained and all
that sat before him was an old Austrian woman. The

two husbands had devoured the living flesh. Now she had to bear her ailing bulk herself.

And even as he said, "I was so glad . . ." as if about to rise, she suddenly pursed her lips, patted her white hair, and the peasant expression vanished from her face; a flush of anxiety, very familiar to him, spread over her hands, as it had at home between one terror and the next. She said, "After the deportation, your Uncle Salo arrived drunk on my doorstep and asked me to hide him, but I was too frightened to let him in. May God forgive me. I should have let him in, but I was very frightened." Strange, thought Bruno, it bothers her.

She went on. "I preferred Salo over all the others." She laughed softly, like a woman remembering ancient sins. "He brought me silk stockings from Vienna and the most expensive eau de cologne. I remember your house well. They knew how to show a woman kindness there. No one ever raised a pitchfork to a woman in your house. I've known the taste of a pitchfork on my thighs," she said, and raised her skirt. "You see."

"But why—why?"

"Because my first husband said that living in the Jewish house had spoiled me and given me airs above my station. No Jew would take a pitchfork to a woman's thighs. Jews love women."

Bruno laughed. "Jews for love!"

"Yes, my dear, believe me, men of good taste who know what's what. Who know how to give a woman what she needs. After all, a woman is God's creature too. God made her with her needs and her desires. I loved your mother too. If only I had listened to her I would never have sunk so low, but there was something wicked in me when I was young. The devil knows."

"You know my whole family."

"Fine, handsome men your uncles were. The sins of my youth come back to me today."

Her ugliness vanished for a moment and she sat withdrawn into herself. The thought that the uncles who

had visited their home in the summertime had enjoyed
the favors of Louise, this secret thought gave him an
agreeable feeling now, like a greeting from far away.

"I'm glad," he said.

"So am I. A lot of good comes back."

She did not ask if any of them had survived. The
little light that had come into her face dulled, and the
pale fat closed over her eyes again. Her hands trembled
like an old woman's on the table.

"There's so much to ask, I don't know where to
begin," he said apologetically.

But there were no questions in his mind. He told
her in detached and rather dreary detail about the long
journey, the local train, and the drunks. He dragged
his story out, in the local German words, chattering on
and on, as if he had just come back from a boring,
cheerless holiday. And when she rose to her feet and
said that she had to go now, he too rose and said that
he would have liked to ask a lot of questions; there
were so many things he wanted to ask about, that in
the end he hadn't asked anything. He was excited,
everything was so beautiful and so familiar. And as he
returned to the subject of the train journey, going into
more and more pointless detail, Louise held out her
hand and said, "As always, I'm a slave to my masters.
I'm working in the sanitation department now." Bruno
bowed to her and with his right hand made a queer,
triumphant gesture in the air.

As Louise receded into the shadows of the avenue
he continued to stand there, overcome by a strange
elation he did not know what to do with. In the south
the light was already changing, and cold shadows were
creeping along the church walls and the fences of the
houses. Louise, he repeated to himself, you knew them
all with your body. Only now, it seemed, did he grasp
that he was here, in the town of his birth, where all the
shadows were familiar and every little movement was
lapped by the rhythm of the water in the stream.

His strange elation wore off, and a naked melancholy, which fed on his flesh, clenched his chest. The

feeling of flatness did not leave him even when he was
sitting in the bar numbing himself with brandy. The
brandy burned his throat with its bitterness. A couple
of drunks sat next to him, laughing and cursing and
cracking jokes.

"How much do you drink?" one of them asked him.

"Six a day," said Bruno quietly.

"Half your salary, I'll bet."

"So what?"

"And you never went to the rehabilitation center for
alcoholics?"

"I would never set foot in a place like that," said
Bruno, with the air of a confirmed old sot.

"And your wife never set the welfare on you?" inquired the drunk.

"No," said Bruno shortly, like one of the locals.

"I beat my wife yesterday until she set the welfare
on me," said the drunk. "They wanted to drag me off
to that dump of theirs."

"I know what you mean," said Bruno, enjoying the
language coming back. "I'd never have gone."

"I don't give a damn for the welfare. But her I
won't forgive in a hurry. Have one on me, for friendship's sake."

"I've had my ration for today," said Bruno.

"You're refusing me."

"Not at all, I'm full up."

"I'll let you off now on one condition," said the
drunk. "The first one tomorrow is on me."

"On my oath," said Bruno.

The day was dying and delicate shadows crept inside
and spread over the floor. The silly exchange with the
drunk tickled the roots of his sadness a little. He
walked along the avenue, breathing in the early evening.
The brandy filled his emptiness and he felt sated. Two
prostitutes in miniskirts were standing on the corner.
They looked shy in their revealing clothes.

The light grew gray and between the trees he could
see shutters coming down over shop windows. Someone
asked the time and a woman's voice answered, "Seven."

The evening with the first electric lights coming on, the tapping heels, and the two shamefaced prostitutes soothed him now, the aftermath of a catastrophe momentarily forgotten. He worked out that it would take him another half hour to reach the inn. When he got there he would have a cup of coffee and read the newspaper.

He thought of Louise, her face opening up for a moment at the sound of the forgotten names and closing again into its sick folds of fat. Now he saw nothing but her upper lip, trembling like a frightened animal. In the café she had broken her cake with both hands as if it weren't cake but some stubborn object refusing to open. When he got back to the inn he did not read the newspaper or drink a cup of coffee. He was overcome with weariness. In his sleep he heard only the chambermaids giggling in the cloakroom and whispering crude words to each other.

6

TWO weeks here already. He leaves the hotel in the morning and in the evening he returns: he puts his head on the pillow and floats into a thirsty sleep on the whispered exchanges of the chambermaids. And when he wakes he cannot remember a single picture from his dreams. And once again he stands in the square, walks down Hapsburg Avenue, and sits on the bench in the public park. No one pays any attention to him and when a sudden rain falls on the town he abandons the bench and stands next to the wall.

The air in this season of the year is both fresh and enervating, but he overcomes his weariness and takes in everything, down to the slightest movement rustling the branches of the trees. At noon he goes into the Old Bouquet of Flowers, to Lonka. Lonka is so old and sick that she doesn't even remember the customers' orders. And when he says, "Coffee with chicory," she mumbles it to herself, "Coffee with chicory," so as not to forget it on the way to the kitchen. In the middle of the day nobody comes into the café. He sits there for an hour or two, sipping coffee and watching the delicate shadows that have not changed their position by the window since his childhood. And when the shadows dissolve he fixes his eyes on the door and waits for a familiar step. The solid door is dumb. The light diminishes and the brown door blackens before his eyes.

But yesterday he noticed a tiny, sudden movement.

177

The shadow of the chestnut tree spread out at the
foot of the bench in a sweeping movement and immediately withdrew, gathering itself back to the trunk of
the tree. This tiny movement repeated itself a number
of times, and then he saw that a man was standing next
to the chestnut tree. Because the man was standing with
his back to him, Bruno thought it was the crazy Brum,
but he immediately realized his mistake. The man
looked familiar but not familiar enough for Bruno to
dare approach him. The man did not stir. His wide
coat swept the shadows into a flurry around him. He
stood there for some time and then turned aside.

The gentle movement of the shadows gave rise to a
certain uneasiness in Bruno, but only superficially. Immediately afterward two women dressed in the old
style appeared. They were talking about some society
that was about to break up, but to Bruno it seemed
they were trying to distract him. He stood up and they
went on talking about the same subject. When he
moved away he heard them clearly: they were talking
about the botanical gardens that had once been adopted
by the parents' committee of the gymnasium. His
mother had been a member of the committee for two
years. Now it seemed that the botanical gardens were
in trouble and the committee was trying to divest itself
of its responsibility. Bruno chuckled as if a soothing
breeze had touched him.

He left the park and strolled down the little lanes.
It was already evening. Domestic sounds rose from the
low, creeper-covered houses, mingled with the aroma
of fresh coffee. Now he felt with new force that everything here, including the little movements of the night,
was known to him. He observed without surprise, like
someone watching a familiar river in a quiet season.
He felt a desire to knock on one of the doors and say,
"I'm here. Don't you remember me?"

Strange. When he was a child he would sometimes
dream that he had come back to his town and no one
knew him. He would wander from place to place,
panic-stricken because of the silent, conspiratorial re-

fusal to acknowledge his existence. He had spent a lot
of time thinking about these dreams then, and their
nightmarish absurdity. There were some remnants of
old converts in the town. But to approach them at this
hour seemed to him even more absurd.

And thus, without thinking, he found himself once
more in Hill's underground cavern. Hill was not there.
Cheap, sticky, melodious music poured from the loud-
speakers. A kind of emptiness, together with the sour
smell of tobacco, hung in the air.

The first drink gave him considerable relief. He was
about to order a second, and as he turned his head he
saw: Hill, and behind her a crowd of youngsters. Except for two girls with them, there would have been
nothing striking about their appearance. It was the kind
of crowd you can see in any bar. They made for the
right-hand corner, where there was a long bench standing against the wall.

"Sit down, brothers, sit down," said Hill. She sounded
like a chambermaid.

As they carelessly flopped down, Hill noticed him.
She came over and said, "You're here. Look at the
tribe I've brought along with me, a tribe of sensitive
young souls. Wouldn't you like to meet them?"

"Who are they?" he asked, taken aback.

"Our kind of people," said Hill with the practiced
ease of a barmaid. "Mongrels of the nicest possible
kind." Hill was in high spirits and announced, "Meet
Bruno from Jerusalem." Her announcement made no
impression. They had come to celebrate Erwin's birthday and were preoccupied with their festivities. But one
thin and sloppy girl with brown beads of sweat shining
on her brow said, "How interesting, Jerusalem."

And without asking permission she sat down beside
him. Her narrow face was without charm. The steel-
rimmed glasses on her nose emphasized the smallness of
her eyes.

"Jerusalem," she said, not addressing him directly.
"What's in Jerusalem?"

"A town like any other," said Bruno coolly.

"And what about the glory and the holiness?" she asked carelessly.

"They're there."

"In that case what brings you here, if I may ask?"

"This is the town I was born in and I came to see it."

"We're all molded from the same clay then, aren't we?"

"And you?"

"I'm just an ordinary mongrel girl, a mongrel without any pretensions." The round glasses glinted on her face with a slightly mocking air. Her secret, obviously, was a well-kept one. She had no desire to speak about it seriously.

In the meantime the bar took on a festive air. The midgets stood next to the counter and tuned their instruments. They looked like children that grown-ups had abused.

"And did you find many old acquaintances here?" She spoke as if she hadn't intended to ask.

"No," said Bruno. "Everything has changed in the years I was away."

"What's your name, if I may ask?"

"Bruno A. Does that mean anything to you?"

"No. Nothing at all."

Her friends were already crowding around the brandy bottle. From a distance everything they said sounded the same. The girl stared at them. It was obvious she was now taking pleasure in observing her friends from a certain distance.

"Suzi, come and see a new man," she called out to a rather fat girl.

The fat girl turned around and with a theatrical gesture said, "Who's calling me? Who's interested in my company?"

"Me," said the girl. "There's a new man here. From Jerusalem. Does that mean anything to you?"

The fat girl stared at Bruno and said, "My name is Suzi. My body tells the truth about me. The man, you say, is from Jerusalem. Interesting. Very interesting. But why, in fact, should it be?"

"What are you saying?" said the other girl.

"Sorry," said Suzi mockingly. "I forgot that there are cities and cities."

"The man is also a native of our town and a member of our race—and, if I'm not mistaken, pure and un-alloyed."

"In that case, I salute him," said Suzi and saluted. "Forgive us for our inferiority. We're only half-breeds, full of imperfections."

The other girl laughed loudly. And Suzi asked, "Why are you laughing?"

"What do you mean, 'why?' At your eloquence."

By now Erwin was already in the embrace of two girls who kept kissing him. The group egged them on and they kissed him noisily.

A kind of sourness seeped through Bruno. His coming here now seemed more pointless than ever. And these young people, grotesque in their gaiety, did not amuse him. He was dizzy from the brandy and his right hand tapped mechanically in time to the music.

"What are you doing with yourself here?" asked Suzi, flirtatious innuendo in her voice.

"Nothing."

"We must look after him." She turned to her friend. "He'll give our town a bad name. He'll say you can't have a good time here."

The party grew louder. The alcohol was apparently having its effect. A tall man recited advertising slogans and they all chorused the responses, stamping their feet like horses. The midgets broke out into melodious songs. Suzi grimaced as though she had tasted something disgusting.

"Can't someone stop them?" she pleaded. "This sentimentality is driving me crazy."

Bruno was about to get up. The music was pressing against his temples. He wanted to be by himself again. How good it had been here last night. There had been no one here. The alcohol had seeped slowly through him and he had felt it working in all his limbs, though on the way back to the hotel an elderly prostitute had accosted him and destroyed the soft web of his thoughts. He had lost his temper and flung a curse at her. But the empty curse had not relieved him and all the way home he had felt a need to vomit.

Meanwhile, as his thoughts babbled on, he noticed the light changing on Suzi's face. She put both hands to her face and stretched her skin tight. The music apparently bothered her and she made the same disgusted face again. There was something painfully familiar in her expression.

"Just a minute," said Bruno, as if he were sweeping away some clutter of objects obstructing his view. "Don't I know you?" He was taken aback by his own boldness.

Suzi turned her head. The familiar expression disappeared. Her graceless ugliness reasserted itself. "Maybe," she said. "I used to work as a chambermaid in the Continental Hotel. And as a night waitress in the bar. I worked for a while in the kitchen, but then they promoted me. And I never descended to the kitchen level again. A checkered career, you might say."

"But what's your name?" He looked at her directly, into her eyes.

"Suzi, I told you. A poor, plain name. To me it means nothing. It's disgusting."

"I meant your family name."

"I see that you're intent on cross-examining me. Why not? I'm used to cross-examinations. So, let me tell you my family name. You must know that I have two. I'll tell you the secret one. My secret name is Suzi Kaufmann. My fathers and fathers' fathers were merchants, they traded in myrrh and saffron and frankincense. Beautiful merchants, sensitive merchants, merchants who brought their merchandise from afar, as they say in the storybooks. Merchants who had beautiful women. Discriminating merchants. What are you laughing at? What's so funny?" And she went on lavishing praises on the merchants until in the end she said, "Merchants like them are every woman's dream."

Bruno dropped his head. The words beat frantically

against his temples. The intuition that the girl sitting in front of him was his Uncle Salo's illegitimate daughter was as strong and clear as a light breaking through fog and turning dim shapes into certainties.

"What do you think of my name? My history lesson? Or perhaps you too shrink from such names?" She continued her attack.

"I once knew a man called Kaufmann." Bruno raised his head.

"In that case you knew my father. He was a Jew. A Jew like you. A Jew who had two women. Because he loved women. And I'm the offspring of his mistress."

Uncle Salo. For years his memory had been buried together with that of his father, in the cold silence of a damp cellar. His jaunty, volatile uncle, who was addicted to women and gave rise to a new scandal every year.

Again Suzi passed both hands over her face, revealing the length of her fingers to him.

"My mother kept the secret for years." Suzi turned to her friend.

"Did it come as a surprise?" asked the girl.

"Not much. I'd always felt there was something peculiar about me. Now I know, now I'm wise."

"Interesting . . . What did they tell you?"

"At first they told me that my father was killed in the war."

"They told me," said the other girl, "that my father was drowned in the river."

"And were you angry?"

"Angry? Why should I have been angry?"

"I," said Suzi, "was furious. I wouldn't speak to my mother for a year."

The midgets sat in a corner and played softly. Bruno felt a sad closeness with the girls. Suzi kept on stretching the skin on her face.

"Where did your Kaufmann come from? Excuse me for asking. After all, I'm his daughter. Illegitimate, it's true, but related nevertheless."

"He was my uncle," said Bruno, almost whispering.

Suzi opened both eyes wide, lifted her right hand, and placed it on the table. A cold astonishment flashed across her face and she said, "Incredible." But immediately afterward, as if she were afraid of herself, she turned to the merrymakers in the corner and announced, "I have thrilling news."

Erwin, in a glow of drunken happiness, heard her and said, "What? What's the news?"

"I've discovered a long-lost cousin."

"Lost to what?"

"Lost to the Jewish part of me."

They all rose to their feet and with lithe steps surrounded the table. Erwin said, "Why don't you kiss him?"

Suzi, without any hesitation, took Bruno's face in her hands and kissed it, and said, "My cousin and flesh of my flesh—my spiritual flesh, if I may put it that way."

"Are you mad?" said the other girl.

But Erwin egged her on and commanded, "Now swear an oath of loyalty to the spiritual part of you. The mysterious part."

"What do you want of her?"

"A declaration of faith," said the drunk emphatically.

Suzi pulled up her skirt, exposing her fat thighs, and said, "My legs have no part in my Jewish mystery."

They brought bottles, poured out drinks, and drank. No one asked him when or how. Suzi gulped down two glasses of brandy, one after the other, and the words came tumbling out. She returned to her previous theme and once more told the story, as in a play for children, of the tall, swarthy, subtle merchants who brought precious perfumes from the Orient.

Erwin said, "My secret name is Hofmann. It means that my forefathers came from a line of princes."

Strange new words, drunken words fluttered in the air, and flung themselves against the gloom. Bruno understood them as one understands cues in a nightmare. And with the uproar at its height, someone else stood up, his face full of sharp lines, and said that he rejected this ceremony with contempt. He, at any rate, would not make a mystical cult out of simple biology. His thin, hooked nose bore witness to considerable polemical powers.

Suzi, surprised, went up to him and said, "What's upsetting you?"

"This adulation," he said quietly.

"I," said Suzi, "wish to make a public announcement that my unknown father is dearer to me than all of Austria. And I go down on my knees to worship him. Like this." And she got down on her knees.

"Not me," said the thin young man. "Not me."

"I," said Suzi, "bow down to the ground, like this, like this, and I say that my unknown father—my father who loved many women—is my love forever."

"Not me," repeated the thin man.

"What do you want of her?" the other girl interrupted.

"I bow down to no one."

"I," said Suzi hysterically, "declare that the Jewish blood flowing in my veins is the vital blood, the beautiful blood, the blood that I love."

The bar owner, who had refrained from intervening up till now, turned to their corner saying, "This isn't a cage at the zoo. Calm down."

This warning from the counter succeeded only in enflaming the hysteria. The possessed and drunken words hovered above them. The girl's pleading fell on deaf ears: "You're spoiling Erwin's birthday party." Erwin himself, divested of the two girls who had been clinging to him, looked clumsy and pathetic without them. Suzi, crouching on her knees, kept on bowing down to the ground and proclaiming, "I prostrate myself to my unknown father."

And since the repeated warnings of the bar owner had no effect, two brawny waiters emerged and wordlessly showed them the door. They left without argument. Bruno sat deserted in his chair. It was seven o'clock and there was an empty silence in the bar. The isolated words impinging on the silence from outside only intensified the emptiness. The delicate melancholy left by the brandy evaporated. And another sorrow, clumsy and heavy, spread through his limbs.

Hill approached him and said, "Wasn't that a nice surprise?"

"Fantastic," said Bruno.

"That's the way they are, our half-breeds. You can't change them," said Hill in a tone of delicate, feminine apology. "But I like them just the way they are."

"Do you know them well?"

"What do you mean? We grew up together. We discovered each other and ourselves. And the bond has remained to this day."

"And Suzi?"

"We grew up together. We sucked the same milk from the same cow, as they say in the country."

The bar owner beckoned her to the microphone and she skipped over to the counter.

With the heavy sorrow still oppressing his heart, he sensed the notes of a delicate melody coming near. He put on his coat and without saying good-bye to Hill he left the bar. The first lights of the night flowed quietly from the windows. There was no movement, only the silent flow of the light. He walked from street to street until he found himself standing outside the illuminated shop of the convert Fürst. Fürst's sturdy grandfather had managed to get himself baptized in the quiet and easy-going days of the Emperor Franz Josef. Although he was loyal to his new religion he did not cut himself off from the Jews. His sons too went on meeting Jews. Everyone said that there was still something Jewish about the Fürsts. Now the grandson sat in his comfortable tobacconist's shop and smoked a pipe, looking like a well-preserved old Austrian whose body had been pampered by drink and tobacco. The shop was empty.

"I'll go in," said Bruno and he went in.

The bell rang above the door as in old-fashioned

shops. A strong smell of alcohol and tobacco hit him in the face.

"What can I do for you, sir?" the old man asked.

"Eden tobacco," said Bruno in his father's voice.

"We haven't had it for years. Where are you from, sir?"

"I was born here in this town. I left it thirty years ago."

"Let me try to remember."

"My name is Bruno A. The son of . . ."

"Let me look at you for a moment."

"Jews." Bruno flung the word into the empty air.

"I understand," said the old man and his old eyes suddenly froze, as if a living monster had been thrown onto the counter.

"What do you say, what do you say?" he said and his hands shook on the counter.

"I was walking past the shop and the smell of tobacco hit me in the face."

"My brother—my brother," cried the old man. "I myself did not have the courage." He mumbled as if he wanted to get down on his knees. But he continued to stand. He stood erect.

"I didn't mean to disturb you," said Bruno. "I've just met my cousin. My Uncle Salo's illegitimate daughter. My Uncle Salo, you must remember him."

The old man gaped as if he were trying to absorb the information through his mouth. Bruno continued. "A wonderful girl. She's not like him in appearance, but her fingers are just like his."

The old man shook. He had certainly not anticipated a nightmare of this order.

"I myself did not have the courage. I'm not asking for mercy. But I myself did not have the courage."

The old man made a peculiar movement as if he were about to bow down, but instead he held on to the tin of tobacco and put it back on the shelf. "I've been here for two weeks already," said Bruno without taking his eyes off the old man's trembling hands. "Two weeks. How glad I was to meet my uncle's daughter.

She's not like her father and yet everything about her is like him."

The old man's face brightened and a mysterious smile spread over his lips. It was only for a moment, for immediately he clenched his trembling hand and beat his fist fiercely on his forehead. "This is the louse. His name is August. This is the louse. His name is August."

For a moment Bruno wanted to take the old man's hand and say that he was sorry. But the old man sensed his intention and said, "No." And Bruno left.

The Fürsts were honest people. A strange honesty. A sick honesty. And in the evil days they stood up to be counted and joined the queue with all the other deportees. The way they stood by themselves in the locked temple stirred the hearts of the beaten people with wonder for the last time. There were four of them and all the way to Minsk they did not remove their caps. Not all the Fürsts possessed the same strength, however. August stayed in his shop. And he was still sitting in it. And all night long Bruno continued to see the converts standing at attention in the temple like reprimanded soldiers. And afterward too, in the cold and close to death, they did not utter a sound.

7

AFTER this the days were all alike and no rain fell. The trees shed their blossoms and a light snow of petals covered the ground, but Bruno himself had lost his serenity. The damp breezes coming from the river did not ease his tension. He would stand for hours looking at the entrance to Fürst's shop. Strange how this shabby doorway riveted his attention now. Several times he had been on the point of going in and asking the old man's pardon, but his legs refused to carry him; and because he did not go in, the doorway drew him like a magnet. As if his secret was buried somewhere inside its darkness. Most of the converts had died. A few of the longest standing survived. Didn't they miss their severed roots? But these were idle thoughts. Only the Fürsts, he knew, only the Fürsts, their strange integrity intact, had chosen death with their eyes open. The rest had coveted life, and they had been absorbed by it.

He met Suzi again in Hill's lair. She hailed him loudly and cheerfully, "My lost cousin, my darling cousin," and kissed him embarrassingly on the face. Her full face, circumscribed by its silver spectacles, was gay as a barmaid's. Her girl friend sat beside her and sniggered, as if someone had whispered an obscenity in her ear. It was afternoon and the bar was empty. Suzi's friend stretched out her legs and put her feet up on a chair and said that when she was a little girl she thought that "bastard" was an affectionate nickname. And when people asked, "Who's there?" she

would say, "The bastard." The children at school liked
her because she was a champion swimmer; later on
they began calling her the bastard fish. "I remember,"
said Suzi, "I used to call you the bastard fish too."
They went on chattering in this way for some time.
Bruno took no part in the conversation. The cold beer
broke his thirst and dulled his senses. His head was
empty of questions or doubts.

Suddenly Suzi's friend turned to him and said, "Why
are you so quiet?"

"No reason," said Bruno, taken aback.

"What have you got up your sleeve?"

"Nothing, nothing."

"In that case, why are you so quiet?"

"Because I've got nothing to say."

"You look like a man with something up his sleeve
to me."

"Don't take any notice of her," interrupted Suzi.
"She's dreaming."

"I'm not dreaming. I'm wide awake."

"What do you want of him?"

"I don't like the look of him," she insisted.

"He hasn't done anything." Suzi tried to calm her.

"Why has he turned up here where no one wants
him? Jews should be more discreet."

"What do you say?"

"I say what my heart tells me to say. I can't stand
Jews. They're so pushy."

Suzi went down on her knees and put both arms
around her friend's body. "Calm down," she whispered. "Calm down."

Bruno rose to his feet. The revolving fan made a
noise like the buzzing of a trapped insect. He made as
if to pay, but Suzi stopped him with an abrupt, sharp
movement and pointed to the exit. "Pushy!" The girl's
voice followed him out in a loud hiss. Strange, that
word did not hurt him. He went out into the street. It
was five o'clock, the low, soft lights padded the pave-
ments. Isolated voices coming from the river were absorbed into the air. From a distance he saw Louise

making her cumbersome way. For a moment he thought of going up to her, but he remembered that the last time they met she had asked, "Are you still here?"

And while he stood there, respectable-looking couples appeared one after the other. It was obvious that they had just emerged from their houses and were on their way to take their afternoon coffee. "That must be Sturz, and there's Fachmann"——Bruno excitedly identified his old classmates. They passed him by. Their mild, bourgeois voices lay on the silence.

But Brum recognized him all right. He sat on the bench leaning comfortably on his cane, looking on quietly from a distance. A kind of smile hovered beneath his moustache. Their eyes locked for a moment and parted again.

That night he returned to Hill's cavern. Hill was hoarse and sad and her small face looked bleak and exposed. It had been stripped bare from the inside. Bruno told her about the incident with Suzi and her friend. Hill told him that the two of them had been in love with each other for years and that the relationship was a difficult one. While Suzi was full of life, her friend tended to be depressive. They lived together in a rented room and their landlady made a scandal every week. What could they do? They were in love. Was it such a sin?

Hill put her hands on the table. Her fingers said more than her face. Limp, exhausted fingers. Bruno now felt a warm closeness toward her, not erotic, and while they sat silently drinking Hill suddenly said, "Isn't there any other place for us but here?"

"What other place do you have in mind?" asked Bruno.

"I don't know. I need some place that would wash me clean. A place without organized entertainment or lust. You understand."

"I'm trying."

"Is there any such place? There must be. Only not for me. Sometimes it seems to me that the Jewish demon is torturing me. If I can put it that way."

"You believe in demons."

"No. My granny used to say that the Jews always suffered and that was why they were kind to other people. My sister Eveline was more of a success than I was. But she wasn't a complete success either. She was married and divorced. Now she owns a perfume shop on Stiefter Street. She's got more guts than I have.

"Now tell me—my granny used to say, 'His eyes beheld the suffering of men and of charity he gave none. At his death they will not say, Righteousness delivereth from death.' Do you understand that? She always repeated that. And another thing I remember her saying was, 'The fathers have eaten sour grapes and the teeth of the sons are set on edge.' What does it mean, 'set on edge'?"

They sat until late at night. Hill talked and Bruno said nothing. Her voice seeped into him drop by drop. The light went out of her face; it looked very bleak. She rose to her feet and said, "Enough. I'm going to bed."

In the doorway she asked, "Have you got a little cash? I'm stone broke. Perhaps you can lend me something?" Bruno offered fifty marks and she did not thank him. She said, "That's too much."

That night in bed he knew that his stay here was coming to an end. Watery green lights lapped his sleep and he floated heavily in them. At the bottom of the river, amid the brown vegetation, lay Brum, long and heavy. His wakeful brown eyes followed Bruno relentlessly. One little push and I'll be miles away from him, said Bruno to himself. And he was about to move off, but when he tried to move his arms he discovered that his hands had put forth roots he could not easily pull up.

8

AFTER this came hazy days. Sitting on the public bench he began to feel uncomfortable. Broad shadows shifted from tree to tree and made him feel uneasy; and although no one addressed him, it seemed to him that he was now known. From time to time he felt glances resting on his coat, then slipping away.

Next to the bakery he met Louise. She asked, "Are you still here?" Her surprise, which was not, perhaps, intended to offend him, gave him pain. She looked like a peasant whose ugly scars were from years of corrupt city living. But not her walk. Her walk was heavy and countrified. She did not ask, "What are you doing?" or "What are your plans?" It was obvious that his presence did not please her. But with Brum he had a couple of noteworthy conversations. Brum was not appeased, but the way he sat indicated a certain readiness for dialogue.

A few days earlier, Bruno met him in the narrow lane by the mill, a beautiful, silent lane filled with the scent of creepers, covered in this season with purple flowers. Brum sat on the bench outside the inn. It was early evening and Bruno was tired from walking around. In fact, he wanted to call it a day and go back to the hotel.

"Good evening, Mr. Brum, how nice to meet you." Bruno challenged him directly.

"Good evening to you," said Brum, a shamed, bash-

193

ful smile settling on his face. His long moustache, for some reason, seemed sparse.

"Do you recognize me?"

"Of course," said Brum. "You are the son of the writer A. I used to be one of your father's admirers."

"And now?"

"Now I admire no one."

There was a sharpness in his voice, as though it did not want to speak but cut.

"Why then do you avoid me?" Bruno was filled with unexpected courage.

"I?" said Brum in astonishment. "Don't I answer your questions?"

Now for the first time he saw him from close up, an old but robust man. A bitter honesty flickered over his face. A few weak traces of his former life were left on his face, almost obscured by his hairy moustache, but one movement, against which he appeared to struggle, came out as a crooked shrug. Bruno was about to turn aside.

"I," Brum repeated, "am not avoiding questions."

Bruno, seeing something conciliatory in this remark, and perhaps even an opening for some kind of exchange, said, "A few days ago I met my Uncle Salo's illegitimate daughter. You must remember him."

"What of it?"

"I was very excited. In general she doesn't look like him but her fingers are exactly like his."

Brum raised his bushy eyebrows and with a disdainful expression he rejected the words that had presumed too much.

"You must remember my Uncle Salo."

"Of course I remember him. He was a wild one." Brum smiled strangely and rose to his feet, as if this idle conversation held no further interest for him.

The next day he met Brum again, not far from the same lane, and this time there was a surprise in store for him.

Brum turned to him and said, "So you're still here."

"A few more days."

Brum seemed to have recovered somewhat. He no longer seemed so bizarre. His broad face expressed the skepticism of an old man whose life had left him empty of faith or aspiration.

"And what have you been doing with yourself?" asked Brum.

"Nothing; walking around."

"Aren't you bored?"

"No. There are places that bring back memories."

And as the conversation proceeded in this vein of wary neutrality Brum suddenly looked him straight in the eye and said, "I wouldn't have come back here."

"Why not?"

"Because the women here are corrupt."

"I don't understand."

"You must be blind. Every one. Every one. My wife, whom I trusted completely, was a whore. Disgraceful. I cast her off. Now do you understand? Never put your trust in a woman. Better take up with a tree, or a dog. Now do you understand? What are you staring at? Don't I speak the truth?"

"I suppose so."

"Don't say you suppose so. I hate that phrase. Woman is treacherous by her very nature." He rose stiffly to his feet and the hidden insanity broke out in his face again. "Don't say you suppose so. I'm warning you."

These unexpectedly acrimonious words depressed Bruno. For a moment he stood there feeling dizzy, as if he were about to bend down and pick up precious objects scattered all over the ground. For a long time he walked back and forth in the twilight, which at this season of the year lasted for hours. The first shadows of the night blossomed on the low walls. Strange, the worthless conversation with Brum gave him no rest. It was only when he stood on the hill, the abandoned hill as they called it, touching the sparse bushes, which even in this burgeoning season would never rise above his knees, that the storm in his breast subsided. It was very quiet. Not a rustle or a bird song. The little brook flowed silver in its narrow bed like a metallic

tendon. He used to come here with his father at the
end of summer. Because they only came here once a
year, the place had remained with him as something
wonderful and unique. To this place his father had
brought Stefan Zweig, Jakob Wassermann, and Max
Brod. They too had been enchanted by the fresh sim-
plicity of the scene. Nothing superfluous. Only the hill
itself and a few sparse bushes. And the little brook too,
as modest as the vegetation.

In the last year the writers did not come and his
father spent many hours with the priest Mauber. Their
conversations were long and exhausting and lasted until
late at night. Mauber thought that the Jews should get
out as quickly as they could and go to Palestine to
make a new life for themselves there. His father, who
had never been enthusiastic about the Zionist idea, rejected this program and argued that it was nothing but
anti-Semitism in a new guise.

The priest Mauber insisted that he was talking about
deep religious longings as well as historical necessity.
The Jews, even against their will, would be the torch-
bearers. The elect. At these words his father would look
as though he had tasted something repellent. But Mauber only repeated that the truth would yet be revealed.
His face was full of fierce conviction, the conviction of
a prophet of wrath.

The last conversation, the worst of them all, took
place here too, on this hill. Everything around them
was already infected with hatred, rejection, and re-
newed discrimination. Of course, no one knew yet where
these things would lead. But the bitter smell was already
everywhere. Mauber begged his father, "Why don't you
leave? Why don't you emigrate to Palestine?" The tone
of his voice was both ardent and practical. And while
the priest persuaded and coaxed, his father took off his
hat and said, "I, for one, will not emigrate. I would
rather be persecuted and disgraced than emigrate. I've
done nothing wrong. I am an Austrian writer. No one
will deny me this title."

Mauber, shaken, bowed his head and said, "I cannot understand your obstinacy." All the way home, along Hapsburg Avenue, they did not speak a word to each other. His father's hand did not stop shaking even when they got home. His mother served fish for supper and when she asked if the priest Mauber was willing to help them, his father said brutally: "I don't live by his mouth."

9

AND suddenly rain, a fine summer rain, came down. Bruno wrapped himself in his coat and set out for town. It was early and there was no one in the square. A few pupils late for school ran down the street in a panic; and apart from them nothing at all. The thin drizzle slashed the avenue into wet strips.

In the last year, between one exam and the next, the satchel heavy on his back, he would drag his feet along this pavement. In the last term the exams were difficult but he passed them all. The high grades he brought home did not make his mother happy. Something of that same dull sorrow, his mother's final sorrow, came back to him now.

He felt the cool air blowing at his feet and pushing him on. Visibility was poor. Despite the mist he saw that the shutters were open in Lauffer's shop and one cabinet was illuminated by electric light. It caught his eye. Strange, he reflected, objects survive longer; they are passive. Otherwise how could they withstand such changes? Could it be said, perhaps, that they lacked sensitivity? While he was standing there the light went out and a thin veil of darkness descended on the display window.

Now he was by himself, in the tepid air that was neither good nor harmful. His coat warmed him and his shoes protected his feet. He walked past the Old Bouquet of Flowers, past the bar; the people he had met now hurried past him, some to the grocer, and some to the baker. The smell of fresh bread rose into the air for a moment and evaporated.

Now he understood: the dense blossoming that had greeted him on his arrival was over. The trees were green. The fruit was ripening. And but for the mist, which did not disperse even in the open square, he would have seen that the summer rains had left dark stains on the walls of the Rosenbergs' house.

For some reason he remembered Suzi, kneeling at her friend's feet and trying to comfort her. How strange and sharp her gesture had been when she asked him to leave. As if she were holding a dangerous dog in her hands. But now, from the distance of a few days, the gesture seemed maternal, a despairing attempt to protect a wild, naughty child. "They love each other," Hill had said. Now he understood the suffering in this bond. Now he understood the look in Hill's eyes when she revealed this cruel secret to him. He walked on, buried in his thoughts. The mist clung low to the trunks of the trees and damp morning light broke through in their upper branches.

While he was still wrapped in thought he saw the Japanese student coming toward him. For some days now he had not met him. He wanted to move aside, but the Japanese was already upon him, short, strong, and unshaven, looking as if he had just emerged from an ugly fight.

"You're still here?" asked the Japanese. Although he tried to make his voice sound natural, it came out weak and devoid of will.

He was leaving Austria the next day. He couldn't stand being alien any more. If he continued his studies it would be in Tokyo. He asked how Hill was and laughed. Two years of his life had been lost here, and Hill too belonged to that loss. Now he would have to make up for lost time. His German was garbled and broken; nevertheless his intentions were clear. He was taking nothing with him from here, not even the memory of Hill. He spoke with a sad sobriety. His expression was stronger than his words. They parted with a handshake. The Japanese crossed the street, his short legs stepping rapidly over the adjacent lane as well.

Without thinking, Bruno found himself once more in narrow Graben Lane. The morning mist had dispersed and the good smell of summer rain was pure and clear in the air. In the inn the owner and his wife were eating. They sat and ate their meal without a word. The man seemed young, about thirty-five, but he looked exactly like the trooper standing at the railway station, furiously shoving people into the crowded coaches. "They are still alive," said Bruno, something he had never said to himself before.

It was already eleven o'clock and he was hungry. Since he was standing next to the buffet, he asked for an omelette and a cup of coffee. The transistor emptied its pulsing music into the desolate vacancy. The proprietor did not trouble himself to be polite—he slapped the plate and cup onto the counter without a word. And it was clear to Bruno that the man was angry and not interested in customers. He sat in the place where he had sat before with Louise. The memory of Louise did not gladden him. He paid and hurried out. The proprietor sent a long, disapproving look after him. For a moment Bruno thought of going back and asking him the meaning of his hostility, but the man turned into the kitchen, leaving the hollow sound of a door slamming behind him.

There was a foul, dank smell in the air. Bruno had forgotten the seasonal haze. The mist dispersed but the clarity did not return. The convert Fürst stood at the door of his shop smoking a pipe. His stance expressed nothing but old age.

He met Hill next to the café. She looked bad, her dress slovenly, and she exuded the air of an insulted barmaid who had been kicked out of her bar. A few days before she had quarrelled with the bar owner. She had been fired; her weary face had the rigid lines of a woman determined but blocked. And since she did not know what to do with her determination she was torturing herself. "There's something evil inside us," she

blurted. Bruno tried to soothe her but she was insistent.
"There's something evil inside us." Now the words
sounded like a reproach. Hill told him, for some reason,
about her life before the bar, about her home. She
hadn't lasted long at the gymnasium. Algebra and
Latin were a nightmare to her. She came home with bad
grades. Her father would holler about the waste of
money. Her mother, who had sick Jewish blood in her
veins, did not live long. And in any case she had no
choice but to go out to work. She had started out as
a waitress in the Continental. To tell the truth, those
were good days. Good like alcohol melting through a
body thirsty for it. But the days that came afterward
had devoured good days until there was nothing left
of them. Bruno tried to distract her and said, "It's all as
familiar as the palm of my hand." His words were
vapid and had no ring, and Hill hardly heard them.
Her bleak face grew pale and the protruding joints of
her fingers expressed a dull sadness.

"You'll find another job," he said. This weak con-
solation ignited a dark, hostile green in her eyes. She
said, "You think they don't know who I am? My father
took care to spread the news throughout the town. No
respectable club would have me, not even as a waitress."

"I'd tell them all to go to hell," said Bruno.

"That's easy for you to say," said Hill.

Bruno had nothing else to say. He rose to his feet
and said, "Let's pay." Lonka took the coins and put
them on the shelf.

"Do you know Fürst?" he asked her in the street.

"The tobacconist?"

"Yes, he's a convert, you know."

"I," said Hill, "don't like digging up other people's
pasts."

And with these words they parted. Hill did not thank
him or ask when she would see him again. Her thin
face was cold and despairing. Bruno did not try to
keep her or ask where she was going. The desire to be
alone, this selfish desire, took him over completely.

For hours he wandered aimlessly. A strange power

seemed stored in his fingers and his steps became lighter and lighter. But for the light he would have dived into the river and swum across it. The rest of the night he spent in the inn.

And while he was drinking and dozing he suddenly saw everything that had been hidden from him all the time he had spent here: Jerusalem. In Ibn Gvirol Street the trees were casting their shadows on the pavement and a cool breeze was blowing down the street. Two old people were about to turn right at the corner of Abarbanel Street. Mina was standing by the window with her eyes fixed on the elderly couple.

The last days in Jerusalem. The quarrelling and the bitterness. Mina sitting on the sofa, her full eyes loveless. The third miscarriage, the worst of all, had stripped her of the remnants of her softness. Her lips were drawn tight and all her movements were measured. She did not make a superfluous movement. But precisely this purposefulness, which was not usual with her, awoke a dormant uneasiness in him. Mina went back to her forgotten thesis. Books and notebooks were scattered over the table. And when Bruno said, "Why don't you rest?" she said, "I don't need any rest." Her full eyes held no love. The autumn passed and the cold winter wrapped her even more tightly into herself. Day by day she detached herself from him. Her feet in the woollen socks only intensified their estrangement. Then came the letters: the praises and acclaim for his father from Vienna. Mina did not say, do this or that. She was absorbed in her thesis. He stopped trying to get through to her.

In February she would come home from the university soaked and wrap herself in a blanket. There was no beauty in the way she sat on the bed. And when he said to her, "I'm leaving," Mina did not ask, "Where?" In her full eyes the colors had frozen and a sharp green light flickered in them.

And so like someone diving into a river he left. Mina accompanied him to the airport. Her eyes did not change color. The green remained, cold and frozen.

"Beer?" asked the waitress.

"Brandy, if possible."

"We don't serve alcohol at this time of night."

"In that case, beer."

Bruno had more and more to drink. And the more he drank the more the other color in Mina's eyes was revealed, the violet he loved so much that it hurt him. Now he understood. Not her, but something in her. All the doctors gathered around her bed. The questions. The look on Dr. Graul's face. When the doctors left she wept. But by the next day, her tears had already dried up, and she had stopped asking for sweets.

At the end of the week he came in a cab to take her home. She walked straight ahead with resolute steps. Her feet in their closed shoes were blue, as if they had been bruised. She did not ask, "What shall I return to?" She went back to her books. Her parents had bequeathed her too much suffering. They had met in Auschwitz. The year after the liberation, Mina was born. They were not young. Mina was born in Naples, on the beach.

"Strange," said Bruno, "we never talked about that." Mina would always say, "What is there to talk about? My parents gave me neither beauty nor glory." Bruno too did not talk much about the past. His father, his father. The wound that never healed.

"What do I owe?" asked Bruno, and went out.

10

NIGHT fell and was washed with the splendor of the river. He stood in narrow Graben Lane at a little distance from the bakery, already feeling that whatever had been revealed to him here was about to return to its hiding place, and as he stood there he noticed a man sitting on the bench in the park. The man sat in silence embraced by the shadows, which wrapped him, as it were, in an additional layer of silence.

"Hallo," said a voice.

Strange, said Bruno to himself. Now that it's all over as far as I'm concerned, what does he want from me?

"It's Brum."

"I'm glad," said Bruno, and his voice sounded as if it came from a transmitter.

And as he was about to approach him, Brum rose to his feet and stood facing him with a resolute air.

"How are. you?" said Bruno. "May I invite you to join me in a cup of coffee?"

"What are you thinking of?" said Brum in a rather mocking tone of voice.

"For old times' sake."

"I have cut myself off from everything that you refer to as old times. All I feel with regard to my former life is disgust."

"In that case, I beg your pardon."

"You are overstaying your welcome here," said Brum in the authoritative tone of a petty official.

This remark, and the calm voice in which it was

delivered, infuriated Bruno and he said, "I'll do as I please." And he immediately added, "We don't live by your leave."

"Yes, you may be correct, but nevertheless it's not right for you to come here and stir up evil spirits."

"Evil spirits, you say?"

"Yes, I do."

"Take that back," said Bruno angrily.

"No, I won't take it back. Ever since you arrived, things have been stirred up. Jews again. All that old nightmare again. Isn't it over yet?"

"No, it's not over," Bruno said angrily. "Not as far as I'm concerned."

"I appeal to your common sense," said Brum. "Don't arouse the evil spirits, don't stir them up again."

"What gall," said Bruno, "and coming from you it's even worse."

"Nothing in your character has changed, I see. The same old Jewish impudence."

When Bruno grasped these words in all their nakedness he rushed at Brum, seized hold of his coat, and said in a voice full of power, "Anti-Semitism from you is something I won't permit. From you I expect a little remorse."

Brum, apparently taken aback by Bruno's aggressiveness, shook off his hand, brandished his cane, and said, "Jews don't frighten me." Bruno, with the insult burning his hands, grabbed the coat again and shoved him to the ground. Brum straightened his legs and leaning on his hands he hissed, "My hatred for Jews knows no bounds." Bruno, his hands charged with a strange power, bent down and hit him in the face. Brum, to his surprise, did not cry out but turned his face away in contempt, as if he were not dealing with a man but with some phantom of the night.

"Now it will be easier for you," said Bruno and stepped back. The night sky illuminated Brum's beaten face. A thin thread of blood trickled over his moustache. "Now you can present your arguments." Brum did not reply, but merely wiped his bloody moustache with his sleeve. His face became ugly. His right eye rolled rapidly about as if it were trying to look into the back of his head. His left eye was still. "Don't get up, lie still," Bruno commanded and walked away.

The same night he packed, cramming shirts and souvenirs into his suitcase until it bulged like a swollen belly. The thought that Brum was lying on the ground in the park did not frighten him. He still felt the peculiar burning in his hands, as if the same alien power were tensing his fingers. He paid his bill in full and tipped the chambermaid separately. The proprietress, jealous of this largesse, said, "Well, Turtel, as usual, luckier than you deserve." Something told him to go back to the park and see if Brum were still lying there on the ground. But he was overcome by weariness and closed his eyes. Sleep came to his rescue in a matter of moments. Early in the morning he took his suitcase and without saying good-bye he set out for the station. He drank his morning coffee in the station kiosk.

The coffee was bitter and he sipped it drop by drop like alcohol. The doors of the warehouses were locked. The first light of morning flickered on the roofs. "The local train comes at six," he heard the waitress say. "*It's all over.*" The phrase came into his head. He felt light, the lightness that comes after a deep sleep, and only his knees, for some reason, felt heavy. He ordered another cup of coffee, added milk and sugar and stirred. The mechanical stirring confirmed somehow that he was leaving. The pastries in the cake stand looked dry but he asked for one anyway. The waitress put it down in front of him and he dipped it into his coffee. It was half past five, and the clear morning light fell delicately from the roofs and spread out on the paving stones. The plaza was damp. Not a memory remained with him. It was as if they had all been devoured and left not even a trace behind.

"When does the train arrive?" he asked.

"At six," said the waitress.

"Is it on time?"

"Usually."

The questions and answers were naked. A thin pain, a remnant of the night before, stabbed his right thigh. He rose, stretched, straightened himself, and turned toward the illuminated platform.

"Brum, you have the right to lodge a complaint against me," he said on his way to the platform. His face smiled of its own accord. Nor were these words his own. He stood still for a long time, empty of thought or feeling. His eyes focused vacantly on the blinking railway signal, waiting for the brass plate to fall and the whistle of the engine to pierce the air.